THE CHLOE FILES

My name is Chloe Everson. I'm a dancer at the Red Lagoon in New Salem, Maine. The things I'm going to tell you may seem impossible, unreal, but they're true. I've seen them with my own eyes. All I can say is be careful...there's evil out there...waiting...

SLIVER OF DARKNESS

Who knows what crimes cripple the minds of the guilty?

Brant Lamont's acting career was on a downhill slide, then one night after a performance he vanished. Was he dead? Alive? Forty years later still no one knows what became of the mercurial actor...or the rising starlet who'd become his mistress. It was as if they'd both walked off the face of the earth.

Until Chloe Everson's world flashes to a bizarre black and white and the specter of one of Lamont's characters, the Sliver of Darkness, visits her in the dead of the night.

But ghostly visitations aren't Chloe's only dilemma, because the New Salem Ripper is stalking the waterfront, butchering prostitutes and young strippers, moving ever closer to an encounter with the object of his obsession...

Chloe herself...

Includes the Bonus Chloe Short Story:
THE TROUBLE WITH FLAPPERS

THE CHLOE FILES #2: SLIVER OF DARKNESS &
THE TROUBLE WITH FLAPPERS
by Howard Hopkins

First print and electronic editions: October, 2008

ISBN 978-0-578-00360-3

Published by Golden Perils Press
www.lulu.com/goldenperils
Email: goldenperils@aol.com

Printed in the United States of America

THE CHLOE FILES

#2: SLIVER OF DARKNESS

by

Howard Hopkins

&

A Bonus Chloe Short Story:

THE TROUBLE WITH FLAPPERS

ONE

Uncolor My World

2:00am...

I woke up in black and white.

And naked.

Ok, you're probably thinking I should have known better than to sleep in the nude after dealing with that plague-spreading demon, Praetallious, a few weeks ago and maybe you're right. But I feel more comfortable sleeping in the buff and it's force of habit at this point. Most nights I'm with Arly, anyway, but he's away for a week at some convention for former cops—I know, how could I stay home and pass up so much fun? Well, it's strictly a Boys' Club thingy (thank God). Besides, it was a warm night. I'd even left the windows to either side of my bed open a crack to let in the late spring air and the scent of lilacs from the bushes planted around the townhouse grounds.

Correction: it was warm when I went to bed. Now, not so much. Now a chill permeated my bedroom, as if when the color drained out of the world all heat bled out with it. I glanced at my forearms; they were covered in gooseflesh, as were my breasts and belly. Oh, and don't let anyone tell you black and white hides pimples. It does not. It makes them look like anthills. Big ones.

It dawned on me suddenly: black and white. Everything was in black and white! I jumped out of bed and grabbed my terrycloth robe, which was draped over a corner chair. I've said it before, there's naked and then there's *naked*. And right now I was feeling frickin' *naked*.

I tied the robe closed and glanced about my bedroom. Shadows swelled in corners; chilled-bone moonlight sliced through the blinds and fell in ivory wedges across the carpet. Everything seemed so…stark, like I'd just stepped into an old movie, and a shiver made my teeth chatter.

It was happening again, wasn't it? The supernatural thing.

Crap on a cracker.

I noticed my heart pounding against my ribs and a distinctly uncomfortable feeling of wanting to pee in my panties—assuming I had been wearing any in which to pee. I'd gotten that feeling way too many times over the past few months and it didn't get any more pleasant the hundredth time around.

And go figure, Puddin' Head was sound asleep and snoring his big fuzzy ass off on the entire right-end corner of my bed like nothing whatsoever was wrong. I guess if you're born with a big yellow fur coat the cold takes longer to sink through. I'm guessing once it did he'd be waking up and grumbling about it for the next few days. As the owner of one trouble-attracting stripper human he expected a number of amenities and heat was one of them.

Another freakin' shiver.

I wrapped my arms about myself and stared at my closed bedroom door, every instinct telling me I should just go back to bed and ignore the chilled noir that had unexpectedly taken over my world.

But I was never very good at ignoring stuff that bugged the hell out of me. I've told you Arly calls me impetuous. Again, I'm proving his point. He'd like that. I wasn't going to tell him.

So I took a step towards the door, the carpet like chilled cream between my blue-painted toes. Except, now the blue nail polish just looked kind of dark gray in the absence of pigment.

I stopped, biting my lower lip, and told myself I was probably just dreaming. I was still asleep in bed and maybe should give up watching classic television and eating cold pizza before turning in.

An annoyed grumble came from the end of the bed and I glanced back over a shoulder to see His Majesty had awoken and was not the least bit happy about the lack of warmth. I wasn't sure whether cats could see color, or no color, as the case was, but I'm sure if he had been able to talk the words that would have come out of his mouth would have turned the room blue.

"Don't look at me, you furry ingrate," I whispered, a little afraid my own voice would attract something I didn't want it to attract. "I didn't ask for this."

He appeared unsympathetic.

"You'd make someone a great ex-husband, know that?" I looked back to the door.

Open it, a voice inside urged me.

Are you frickin' crazy? another shot back.

I'm pretty sure the second voice held the advantage. But of course that's the one I ignored.

I drew in a deep breath, took another two steps and gripped the handle. It was cold, and came with the oddest sensation. I don't exactly know how to describe it, but it was like touching...film, maybe.

Bracing myself, I opened the door.

TWO

Things that Go Bump

*T*hings escaped...

Genie Lansing's warning in the church the day we'd confronted Praetallious drummed through my mind as I pulled open my bedroom door. Apparently when Arly disposed of Angelique Ficatier and her Sisters of the Snake a bit before Christmas, certain demons had been lurking at the threshold separating Earth and Hell. When he'd sent Angelique and Czcarabus, the demon the Sisters of the Snake were attempting to resurrect, back to the pits those demons had seized their opportunity to escape, the late, not so great Praetallious being one of them.

But there were others, which was about as comforting as discovering your thong had snapped in the middle of a lap dance.

Was that what I was dealing with again? One of those demons? Had one of them turned my entire world into an old movie?

"So much for my vacation from Evil," I groused in a whisper, more as a tension release than anything else. It didn't work, because when I pulled the door open I almost let out one of those mouse-across-your-feet bleats for no reason other than I was strung tighter than Britney Spears on a Starbucks run.

The hallway was empty, shadows somehow all the more sinister in the colorless gloom. Diffuse moonlight bled into the hall from my bedroom but helped little. I took a step forward, behind me Puddin' Head still voicing his displeasure with the heat situation loud enough to make me wish I was in a *silent* movie.

"Shhh!" I hissed, but he ignored it. He always does. In fact I think it was just an invitation to do it louder.

The hall carpet felt icy between my toes, the same way the bedroom rug had. The hallway appeared longer than usual, endless, a gray-screen optical illusion, probably, each dark patch alive and clutching. My mind started filling the shadows with ebony faces and glittering anti-light eyes. I knew it was only my imagination but I managed to do a damn good job of scaring myself silly by the time I reached the top of the stairs at the end of the hall. I suddenly wished I had the metal pipe I used to prevent the living room slider door from being forced open.

Because when it came down to it, I was basically just a naked girl in a robe, and even though I had started taking a karate class last week, I knew just enough to get myself killed.

I poised at the top of the stairs for what seemed like endless moments, peering down into the darkness of the stairwell. Something about the whole black and white thing just made it all look creepier. Again it ran through my mind that I was always cursing the brainless twits in horror movies who went down into the cellar or up the dark stairs when there was a guy in a hockey mask carrying a meat cleaver loose in the house. I would have to stop yelling at the screen because here I was doing the exact same idiotic thing and it wasn't even the first time in the past few weeks.

I grabbed the handrail and took a step down. The muscles to either side of my jaw ached and I realized I had been clenching my teeth.

Two more steps and I froze.

A laugh whispered up from below, a shuddery sibilant thing, like snakes murmuring. An odd wave a depression came with it, washing over me.

Oh, crap. Crap, crap, crap.

I clutched the rail tighter and my fingers and forearm started to ache. For a moment I couldn't force myself to take another step.

A memory flashed through my mind and made my stomach drop. It was my sixth birthday—well, our sixth birthday, me and my twin sister, Patricia. We had a playroom in the cellar of our ranch house. My father had remodeled everything, right down to the pine paneling and cheesy suspended ceiling panels, and Pat and I had toy boxes and even a small vinyl Wonder Woman tent set up down there. It was early evening and Pat, being Pat, got the bright idea of turning off the cellar lights. I had been playing in the tent and hadn't suspected anything—till everything went dark and I heard giggling.

Pat wasn't afraid of the dark. She and I differed there because I had pretty much instantly peed my pants. I hadn't dared move, but could hear noises outside the tent, all those little sounds you aren't aware of until somebody shuts the lights off on you and you're scared out of your wits.

A lot like waking up in the dead of night to the sound of a burglar downstairs. That same slithery feeling in the pit of your stomach.

That night I hadn't left the tent until my parents came looking for me but by that time I was a crying wreck. Pat actually got a spanking for that one, which pleased me more than it should have.

I felt the same way now, looking down the steps and hearing the shivery laugh. Like I wanted to stay in the tent until somebody came and got me.

But nobody would come this time, would they? Arly was away and it was for damn sure Puddin' Head wasn't about to risk his furry little butt saving his owner. Too many of the neighbors fed him scraps, so he had options.

I did not.

It was go downstairs to investigate or wait until whatever made that laugh came up after me.

THREE

When You Look into the Abyss...Carry a Pipe

I made it down to the landing above the sunken living room before my heart started beating again. I debated charging over to the kitchen to grab a butcher knife from the rack above the counter, but my feet seemed grafted to the carpet.

Moonlight stabbed through the living room slider doors, icy and white, illuminating the sectional couch, glass coffee table, hooded fireplace and overstuffed chair, television set. I was suddenly thankful I'd moved all the boxes I'd packed till Arly and I got married into the storage facility on the townhouse grounds. That left fewer things for anybody to hide behind.

I did notice the slider was closed, the pipe still in place. So no one had broken in that way, unless they were a considerate burglar and replaced the pipe after entering. No monkeys, either, so I was glad for that.

Wait a minute.

The television set.

My gaze jumped back to it and it came crashing home that that wasn't *my* TV set. It was bulky, a big cabinet model thing, like the one I remembered my parents owning when I was little. They'd gotten the beast from my grandmother before she passed away and she'd had it since the early '60s. The damn thing worked nearly 16 years before blowing its picture tube.

In fact, it looked like the exact same set, right down to the dark wood panel doors that slid across the screen.

What the hell was it doing in my living room?

I made my move, then. Without even thinking about it and partly distracted by the alien TV set in my living room, I bolted for the slider, fully expecting cold dark hands to reach out and grab me before I got there. But that didn't happen. I made it to the doors, scooped up the pipe and whirled, ready to face whoever—*whatever?*—had made the laugh.

But again...nothing.

I still couldn't pry my heart out of my throat. My legs had a syrupy feeling I really hated. I remember getting that very same feeling one night when I was stripping. Normally, like I've told you, stripping gave me a sense of control over men. But there was this one guy...

This happened before I started dating Arly, 'bout a year before, I think. This weird guy had come into the Red Lagoon and I knew from the first look he gave me—you know, like some kind of snake looking at a mouse—some of his lights weren't on. He sat himself right next to the stage and just kept staring throughout my entire routine. I dreaded the fact he might pull out a dollar and try to stuff it in my G-string, but fortunately that didn't happen. He had other things on his mind.

Pete—he owns the Lagoon—had walked me to my car that night. He walked all the girls out after I told him about the guy, who incidentally hadn't left until just before closing.

It turned out my instincts were right. The guy was waiting in the back lot when Pete and I came out. He didn't expect Pete to be with me and Pete had a Louisville in one hand, so the guy had made no moves and Pete told him in no uncertain terms never to show his face around the Lagoon again.

Three days later the guy's mug ended up on the news. Same night he had come in, the police found his girlfriend—or I should say parts of her—scattered along the waterfront. She was a former stripper and apparently not the first of his live-ins who had either gone missing or turned up dead. I'd heard about a year back he'd hanged himself in his cell. Good riddance, was all I could say.

I jerked from the memory to find myself squeezing the pipe so hard my hand and wrist throbbed. And positive that stripper-killer's demon soul was suddenly going to be standing in my living room. It was an irrational thought, maybe, but I couldn't shake it.

I listened, afraid to move, the drumming of my own heart and the thundering of my pulse beating in my ears. Anyone human had damn few places behind which to hide in the open layout of my apartment, except perhaps in the shadows behind the counter. I could see both sides of the sectional and nobody was crouching there. Of course, if it were another one of those escaped demons...well, hiding wouldn't really be a problem, would it?

What about the TV? Ok, that was a possibility. Maybe someone could hide behind the big cabinet model that had somehow gotten into my living room.

All right, I told myself, trying to bolster my nerve. You've faced witches and demons and gropers, get hold of yourself...

Right. It was that easy. Let me tell you, no matter how many times you run into ghosties and ghoulies...it *never* gets easier. Maybe it even gets worse because you start expecting them to turn up everywhere.

I forced in a breath and eased to my left, around the couch, towards the TV. I swear if the phone suddenly rang the way it had when the monkey showed up on my patio I was going to smash it with the pipe.

By the time I reached the TV, I had just about worked myself into a panic. It's amazing the things your mind can conjure up when you're scared out of your wits. But probably no more frightening than some of the things Arly and I actually ran into.

No one was hiding behind the TV and I have to say that was only a marginal relief. Because if something *human* had been there at least I could have brained it and only have to worry about getting the blood stains out of the carpet.

But the fact that my apartment was empty...that made things worse, didn't it? And I knew that would be the case because Gibson's Antiques wouldn't have suddenly delivered an old cabinet TV in the dead of a black and white night.

I stood there, staring at the TV, wondering if maybe I should just hit *it* with the pipe. I really wanted to hit something. It would have made me feel a hell of a lot better. Really, it would have.

But that TV was here for a reason, wasn't it? Just like the black and white panorama of my night world. Evil was playing games again. Giving me pieces of a puzzle without a box-cover picture to work from.

I angled around to the front of the TV set and, casting a last glance about my moonlit apartment to make certain nothing would jump out at me, knelt and set my pipe on the carpet. I flexed my fingers, getting the cramps out of my hand, then touched the knob on the sliding panel door. The knob felt exactly the same way my bedroom door handle had. Filmlike, chilled.

"I know this is a bad idea..." I whispered to myself, pulling the panel open.

I was right because the TV screen lit up and scared the living crap out of me.

FOUR

A Horse is a Horse, of Course, of Course

Ok, I should know better than to touch strange objects that appear in my townhouse apartment. It's not like I haven't had previous experience with that sort of thing and that it hasn't always come back to bite me in the ass. Even though no monkey delivered the cabinet model RCA, someone certainly had, and that someone—or something—might still be here or have some message to impart I really had no desire to hear with Arly so far away.

Yet, like an idiot, that's exactly what I did—touched it.

When the screen lit up I flew back onto my ample assets and tried to scramble backward on palms and heels, like the thing was going to form a giant mouth and take a chomp out of me.

No such thing happened, but I am not entirely sure that wouldn't have been better than what did occur.

On the screen was a newscaster from NSN—New Salem News, which as far as I knew hadn't been in existence since the '70s under that name. His voice came hollow, echoy.

"President Kennedy spoke today at a news conference in..."

Whoa! What? President who, now? Kennedy?

Uh-oh. I didn't like the sinking feeling that hit the pit of my stomach. Not one bit. President Kennedy. That would mean that newscast was coming from somewhere between 1961 and '63?

Was that some kind of a joke? Had Evil developed some perverse sense of humor since the last time I met up with It?

The newscaster went on, relaying events that seemed somehow familiar to me, things that I had read about in history books in school—well, at least during the infrequent times I bothered showing up for class.

Even the newscaster himself looked older than the news babes they have nowadays, more mature and businesslike. The delivery was straighter as well, no hyperbole and bluster.

I came back up onto my knees and, against my better judgment but too impetuous to stop myself, crawled back to the TV. That trait was going to get me killed one of these days. I hoped it wasn't tonight.

I touched the channel selector, a big dial thingy with gold numbers etched onto plastic. This bad baby wasn't set up for cable, obviously, but at least Evil hadn't bothered with rabbit ears. Those were a bitch. There was probably some sort of Devil Satellite Signal or something.

I turned the channel. A horse. In a barn, sticking his head out through the top half of a door. And a theme song.

"What the hell?" I whispered. "*Mister Ed*?"

Gee, Wilbur.

Oh, that was just peachy. From President Kennedy to a talking horse…things that had occurred over 40 years ago.

I switched the channel, praying I'd be able to get that damn theme song out of my head sometime in the next century.

A shadowy figure drifted across the screen and some sort of eerie theme music rose up. I didn't recognize the show, but an announcer suddenly came on:

"Who knows what crimes cripple the minds of the guilty? The Sliver of Darkness reveals…"

Ok. This was a new one, at least for me. The theme music crescendoed, swirling and eerie. Some kind of crime show, I figured. I tried to change the channel again but the next station was playing the exact same show. And the next.

Then the screen snapped like a magnified sock shock and went black.

I let out an expletive and thumped the top of the cabinet. Ow. That hurt. And the TV didn't come back on.

I got the feeling I had been shown whatever it was I was supposed to see, given the clues ready to be given.

A laugh shuddered through the semidarkness of the living room and I started, nearly coming out of my skin. I grabbed my pipe and jumped to my feet, whirled.

"Who are you?" I yelled, my voice steadier than I expected it would be. "What do you want? What were you showing me?"

The laugh answered, a whispery slithery thing that sent chills down my spine. It dawned on me that laugh was the same laugh I'd heard on the crime show I had just seen a glimpse of.

That laugh. A sliver of darkness...

It vanished. As inexplicably as it had come. And with it went the black and white. My living room, like that old unfurling NBC Peacock, was now in living color. I turned, saw my own TV set had replaced the cabinet floor model.

I darted to the light on the end table and switched it on. The glare stung my eyes. The heat came back, too, flooding the apartment with the warmth of a balmy, late spring night.

A grumble sounded from the direction of the stairs and I swung my head in that direction. Puddin' Head sat on the bottom step, giving me the hairy cat eye. His displeasure at having been woken up at two in the morning cold was not exactly subtle.

"What?" I said, his stare making me feel somehow like it was *my* fault the supernatural had shown up on my doorstep again.

Oh, wait...I had to give him that point, didn't I?

Because something eerie *had* come to me. Again. And I got the distinct impression it wasn't going to be leaving me alone until I found out what the hell it wanted.

FIVE

Good Eggs, Bad Eggs

6:45am...

By the time I pulled into the New Salem Diner parking lot I was wishing I had gotten some sleep after the mysterious events that had taken place in my apartment last night. But I hadn't. Or, more accurately, couldn't. Waking up in a colorless world had freaked me out quite enough, but possessed television sets? That was pushing it.

I wish Evil would just use the front door. But, no, It had to slip in an air vent or sneak up the cellar stairs. I grew more convinced by the day Evil enjoyed the game as much as the prize. And I had no idea what the game or the prize was in this case.

Puddin' Head hadn't much appreciated the intrusion, either. Believe me, I had heard about it for an hour afterward, and he wouldn't have let me sleep even had I been able to. Fortunately, I had a secret weapon for those times His Majesty got his whiskers in a bunch. I'd waited the hour to give it to him, because I had the weird idea he was playing me, but even so I owed Fancy Feast a letter of thanks for shutting up my cat when all else failed.

But back to point, I was dragging when I got out of my Cherry-red Beretta after pulling into a parking space. Early morning sunlight glinted off the diner's big windows and the speakers spaced about the parking lot. Yes, I said speakers. The diner was one of those retro places that had these old-fashioned metal box speakers for ordering, then a waiter brought your meal out to you on a tray that clipped to the car window. It suddenly occurred to me maybe retro wasn't the best idea, considering my experience last night, but it was too late to change my mind. I'd already gotten Johnny out of bed an hour early to meet me here. It's a good thing he was divorced and didn't have to explain a busty blonde calling at four in the morning to his wife.

I grabbed my jean backpack and slung it over a shoulder. The day was warm, so after showering and pulling my hair back into a ponytail I had slipped into old jeans and a blue blouse just tight enough to make guys trip over themselves. Oh yeah, the power of curves was a good thing.

Unless you were dealing with evil witches, then, not so much.

My legs felt filled with lead as I headed for the glass doors of the diner and my whole body had that weird heavy sensation you sometimes get after one too many Margaritas. Not that I have done that. Often.

The parking lot was empty except for a couple of trucks with out-of-state plates, drivers who had likely been on the road for days and were probably more tired than I was, and Johnny's car.

I had half a thought that as soon as I stepped into the diner everything was going to go all black and white again, but fortunately that didn't happen and saved me the trouble of having to drive home for a clean pair of panties.

I scanned the few faces in the place, all of them looking haggard and sleepy-eyed, or just plain bored with having to go to whatever jobs they held after they finished their breakfast. The air smelled of bacon and coffee and the food was good enough—I'd been here with Arly the couple of times I could drag his butt out of bed early and since the place stayed open twenty-four hours to catch the stripper business from the Red Lagoon I had wound up here a few nights on my own. They did make the best BLTs. But I wouldn't recommend using the restrooms. Take my word on this. If you really can't hold it…hover over the seats. Do *not* sit down.

Johnny—Detective John Sturdevant for those of you who don't know, Arly's friend on the New Salem PD—was sitting in a blue-vinyl-covered booth towards the back, head low, staring into a cup of coffee. I noticed he had the entire pot on the table. He knew what was coming and had taken precautions.

He looked up as I approached and a frown burrowed into his face. Oh, yeah, he knew what was coming, all right. And I couldn't really blame him for dreading it. He was, or at least used to be, a no-nonsense type of cop. But the things he'd seen, and knew Arly and I had seen…well, they were getting to him.

"You're a big bundle of cheer this morning," I said without a lot of conviction, as I slipped my backpack from my shoulder and tossed it onto the booth seat. "Smile, Evil hates that."

He made roughly the same sort of sound Puddin' Head had made last night when he woke up freezing his kitty bits off. And now that I think about it, their expressions weren't a hell of a lot different, either.

"It's not that I don't enjoy seeing you, Chloe," he said, getting little dibbits in his brow. "But every time you or Arly call nowadays..."

I plunked into the seat, not at all happy with the *whoosh* of air it made deflating under my assets. "It's just that I'm right up there with the Angel of Death or a Jehovah's Witness knocking on your door..."

"Your words..." He shrugged.

"I couldn't get hold of Arly during the night. They said he was out with some of his cop buddies somewhere. You were next on the list."

"Maybe he was at a strip joint."

Now why did that make me jealous? Oh, yeah, 'cause that's how Arly had met me and I knew how some of those girls could be. "That's hilarious, Johnny. Maybe you should think about a career in stand-up."

He chuckled, but it was a tired chuckle. "Not sure Ellen needs the competition."

I noticed an extra mug was on the table, so I poured myself a cup of coffee and took a sip. I'd already downed a couple of cups before leaving the house and I think the coffee was the only thing keeping me awake. That and the fact that I suddenly had to pee pretty frickin' bad because if it, but no way in hell was I going to chance using the restroom here.

"So what is it this time?" he asked, and I could tell from his tone he really didn't want the answer. "Warlocks? Werewolves? Tinky Winky?"

"*Mister Ed,*" I said, not really knowing how to start the conversation or what in fact good it would do telling him about it. I was pretty sure he couldn't help but I needed to talk to someone other than my cat, since Arly wasn't available right now.

Note to self: Question Arly about strip joints.

"*Mister Ed?*" I think I might have seen relief on his face. But it was a pretty safe bet that was going to change. "The talking horse?"

"Of course, of course..."

He laughed. It carried a nervous edge but it was a laugh nonetheless.

"It won't be funny in a minute," I said.

He nodded, frowning. "Not that that surprises me at all but what about Mister Ed's got you calling me at four in the morning?"

"He was on TV…last night…"

He shrugged. "I'm only on my first cup of coffee. You're going to have to be a little more specific. What do old '60s reruns have to do with getting me out of bed so early?"

My turn to frown. I wasn't being too clear and I think it was because I was so tired my head was filled with whippoorwills. "Let me start at the beginning."

His expression didn't change, but he took a sip of coffee, then said, "This *is* going to be another one of those things I don't like, isn't it? I knew it. Something to do with what Lansing told you, that there were other…*things* running loose."

I nodded and he let out a heavy sigh. "I woke up last night around two o'clock and everything was in black and white. And cold."

"Black and white? You mean the TV show? That was always black and white."

"No, I mean everything. My room, my body, my entire world. Absolutely no color."

"That's not possible." He said it too quick, like he knew in New Salem it certainly was possible but didn't want to admit it to himself. No matter how much weird crap he saw he still had his cop's need to put a logical explanation to things and deny the supernatural.

"You know better than that, Johnny. I'm telling you everything was in black and white…" I explained everything that had happened, ending with the TV set showing old news clips and a talking horse show. "It was like it was being broadcast as it happened. Like I had stepped back into the early '60s."

"1961," he said.

"You know the year?"

"*Mister Ed* first started as a syndicated program in January of 1961, before going to CBS in October of that year. It was the first midseason replacement show. The horse was a palomino American Saddlebred. There's an urban legend that says if you play the theme song backwards it has a Satanic message, 'The source is the Devil'."

Johnny didn't surprise me often but he did just then. I think Johnny was a closet *Mister Ed* fan. I wasn't thrilled about anything with a Satanic message supposedly involved. I'd just dealt with one urban legend a couple weeks back, and that was quite enough. "And you know this how?"

He squirmed in his seat and I think maybe his cheeks got a bit of red to them. "There's a club…" His voice came out a lot lower.

"A club?"

"Just go on with your story…"

I arched an eyebrow and gave him a cocky nod. "Uh-huh. Any-hooooo, this other show came on afterward…it was strange, nothing I had ever heard of. And it sounded just like the laugh I heard when I came downstairs."

He leaned back in the booth, frowned very deep. "What was it?"

"Something called *Sliver of Darkness*. Looked like some kind of detective show."

He nodded. "'Who knows what crimes cripple the minds of the guilty…'"

"That's it. You know it?"

Another nod. "I've heard of it, but Arly may be able to tell you better on that one. It was a short-lived knock-off of the old radio show, *The Shadow*. The lead actor was Brant Lamont, a local who had made it big. He even did a reproduction of one of the shows at the New Salem Theater while they were still finishing the place."

"He's from New Salem? Is he still alive?"

Sturdevant shook his head and a funny look came into his eyes. "Don't think so. He…he just went missing one day. I think there was some foul play suspected but since they never found a body nothing was ever proved. I don't know all the details."

"Why does that worry me?"

"You think maybe this Lamont was trying to reach you? Give you some sort of message?"

"I'm not sure. At first I thought it was another of those things Lansing told me about, but maybe it's just a ghost."

"Aw cripes, Chlo. Just a ghost?"

"Well, it's better than a demon, right?"

His brow arched. "I have to choose?"

"I think it chose me. But I don't know why or where to go next."

"Can't you just ignore it?" Distressed hope played in his eyes.

I gave him a look of "Yeah, right." "You really think that's an option? I mean, after what just happened a few weeks ago?"

His sigh fluttered a napkin. "I suppose not. You get into more trouble than Arlo. He's not gonna be happy about you pursuing the Big Weird while he's out of town."

"He's gonna be unhappy about a lot more than that if he was out at a strip joint, but Evil does seem to have a bad sense of timing, doesn't it?"

"Or a good one." He took another sip of his coffee. I noticed Johnny was starting to look older than his age. I couldn't help but think that Arly and I were somehow partly responsible for that, but of course Evil got a big part of the blame.

"Can you get me information on the Lamont case?"

"I can, but it will take me a bit of work to dig it up. You might find more on the Internet. There's a fan club."

"Right with the *Mister Ed* one?"

"Don't tell Arlo that."

I grinned. "My lips are sealed."

"Why don't I believe you? You know I'd never hear the end of it." He paused, glanced out through the window at the brightening parking lot. "You find anything else on your sister?"

My stomach tightened and deep sadness welled inside me. "Nothing. I checked back with the Priest at St. Luke's, but he wasn't particularly helpful. He didn't want to talk about Father Lansing's death or where Sister Patricia might have gone. And Arly couldn't get anything out of him, either. It's like he just wanted to keep it all under whatever rug it had been swept. The secretary shut up, too. The priest must have reprimanded her for what little she told me."

"I'll see if I can get any leads on it for you, but since it involves the Catholic Church I wouldn't hold my breath."

I played with a spoon, turning it over, then back again. Sometimes I wondered if I should just give up, let Pat go, but after what happened a couple weeks ago and seeing her ghost... "I went back to St. Bosco's. I didn't tell Arly. There wasn't much left after the fire."

"Something will turn up. At least now you have a direction."

"But still no leads. Every time I go to the museum to talk to Lansing she's not in and she doesn't return my calls."

His expression darkened. "Mmm."

"What is it?" I asked.

He looked back to me, ran a hand through his hair. "Lansing. I looked into her some..." The look got even darker.

"And?"

He shook his head and pulled a stick of Juicy Fruit from his shirt pocket. "I dunno. I ran a check, but..."

"But what? What did you find?" He really didn't have to answer me. I knew what he'd found: nothing.

He unwrapped the gum, stuck the piece into his mouth and gave it a few chews. "She seems to have no real background. I found some things, but they looked..." He shrugged.

"They looked what?"

"Made up. What little there was looked made up. She seems to have attended a catholic school in France before coming to the States, but when I contacted the school there they had no record of anyone by that name, at least not in the past fifty years. Records said she was adopted by military parents, American citizens, but—"

"You couldn't find a record of the parents," I answered for him.

"No, none. And damn little else. I'll keep checking, but I have a weird feeling about Ms. Lansing."

"If you had been in that church with her you'd have gotten an even weirder feeling. It's like she just appears and disappears. And she says her monkey's been dead for 600 years."

"That's impossible." He didn't say it like he believed it.

"I think we've established impossible doesn't really apply in New Salem."

"Maybe I'll send animal control over and see if she's got a permit for the monkey."

"I think a 600-year-old monkey is grandfathered..."

He flashed me a look that said he wasn't amused, paused. "I'm thinking of transferring." His statement came out of the blue and he looked back out through the window as he said it.

"What? What are you talking about? From New Salem?"

An uneasy laugh trickled from his lips. "Like I've told you, I'm just a practical cop. This supernatural stuff...if it's going to keep happening, and I have a strong feeling it is...I don't know if I can take it anymore, Chlo." He looked back to me, a plea in his eyes. "I want my old life back, the one where I went after regular bank robbers and abusive husbands."

I nodded, knowing what he meant and sympathizing. But that didn't change anything. "Sometimes things choose us, Johnny. If I had my choice...I'd be married to Arly now and we'd have a normal life, too.

But I know that's not going to happen, at least the normal part. And I know I can't run from it." I leaned back, sighed. "I don't know what's in our future, and maybe it'll kill Arly or me or both of us, but I have a feeling there's no escape. Arly feels the same way."

"I'm just a cop..." he tried to protest. "You speed, I give you a ticket, You pee in public, I arrest you."

"You haunt a house, a stripper calls you and gets you involved..."

He uttered a soft laugh. "I got kids. I know I don't see them anywhere near enough, but I've got an obligation to them. I know my job took apart my marriage."

"And leaving would help that how? You've got your cop duty, Johnny, but if there's supernatural things threatening to take over this town, maybe this world, you won't be able to run from them. There's nowhere to go. Nowhere far enough, or hidden enough. And you have a duty as a father to protect your kids as best you can. That means accepting some things you won't want to accept. Like demons with plagues, and witches. I tried running away from things after my parents died. You might even say I spent most of my life running till I met Arly. I won't run anymore. It led to nothing but loneliness and the feeling that I was missing out on everything my life was s'posed to be."

"I'm missing out on being with my kids, Chlo. I thought I could handle it. I thought I could be cop and be away from them and it would be ok. I thought I could give custody to my wife because she was there for them. But I'm missing out on everything." He swallowed hard. "The other day my daughter calls and leaves a message on my machine. I had forgotten about her violin recital because I was focused on catching some idiot who held up a convenience store."

"Leaving won't help that. And you might have to sacrifice some things to make sure they are safe long term."

He shook his head, met my gaze. "Don't see a petty thief as a good enough excuse anymore."

I smiled, leaned forward and reached across the table, taking his hand and squeezing it. "But we're not really talking about petty thieves, are we, Johnny? We're talking about running from things, avoiding them, things we don't understand and things that scare the hell out of us. If you leave it won't get better for your kids, it'll get worse. Cut back on your hours, spend more time with them instead of running because you're too afraid to admit you miss them and your old life. Because you're too afraid you can't protect them from the things you don't understand."

"I made a mistake, Chlo, giving them to my wife. I thought it would be for the best."

"You did what you thought was right at the time. Things change. And I have the feeling they've changed because of what you and I have seen. Somehow darkness is shining a light of what's really important in our lives."

He nodded, eyes watering, his gum chewing getting faster. I pulled my hand away.

"I've thought about calling her..."

"Her?"

"My wife. I've thought about maybe trying to talk to her, see if there was a chance..."

"Maybe there is."

"I don't want to die alone, Chlo. When I saw Arlo in the hospital after you rescued him from Praetallious...all he could do was talk about you and if he had died at least he went out loving you. I thought...I thought, what if something killed me tomorrow? What if some supernatural freak or just some idiot with a gun and a mad-on at the world killed me tomorrow? I'd die alone."

Tears welled in my eyes. I could feel the pain in his voice. "Then call her; talk to her and cut your hours. If there's any chance to make it work, take it. And if it doesn't, find someone else before you're looking back at a lonely wasted life."

"I'm afraid I'm already at that point."

I shook my head and stood, grabbed my backpack. I went to his side of the booth, leaned over and kissed him lightly on the forehead. "No, you're not. You're at the part that makes you ask the hard questions. Now make the hard decisions to go along with them." I smiled. "I'll get the check next time..."

I walked away, wondering where the hell I got off giving relationship advice but a little bit proud of myself, too. Maybe I was better at giving advice than taking it, but maybe I also knew the few things in my life I had gotten together were the ones that were going to last the longest.

SIX

On the Radio, Whoa Oh Oh Oh

I understood where Sturdevant was coming from. I really did.

I was driving back to my place, the car window partially open to let in the warm morning air. If it weren't for what I had gone through last night I might have actually felt content.

Because despite the fact Evil was trying to crap all over me, for the first time since my parents died and I lost my sister I had some anchors in my life. Arly was the biggest one. Since meeting him and getting engaged...well, what can I say? When you finally find that person who's meant to be your other half...yeah, I know, that sounds like some sort of silly fairytale but every girl has that dream, whether she wants to admit it or not. From a stripper like me to Martha Stewart. Well, maybe not Martha Stewart. I don't know what's up with *that* woman. Arly was the stability in my life; he had been all through that Sisters of the Snake ordeal and even more so since he proposed. At least, I'm pretty sure he proposed; I was in a coma at the time, but I woke up to find a ring on my finger. Without him, I seriously don't know what I'd be doing now. Stripping, yes, but right before I met him I'd been struggling with a lot of doubts, most of them centered around my life, or the lack thereof.

I was 36—thanks a heap for telling everybody that, Johnny—and even in New Salem there was a limit to the age at which guys were willing to pay to see a gal get naked. It was more and more a young woman's game. Most of the girls coming in were barely 18 and racked up to their chinny-chin-chins with saline. Let's face it, once you hit 30 things started heading south, no matter how much time you spent in the gym.

But I was still pretty decently put together for an old broad, so I guess that isn't the point. The point is you get to this place in your life where you need something more and even though the Big Weird was taking pot shots at Arly and me, I had that something more, though I think I'd been put on official notice I was going to have to protect it.

Johnny didn't really have that. Since his divorce he'd had no anchor and this whole bogeyman thing was causing him even more problems because of that fact. Yeah, sure, he was a no-nonsense cop guy, the way he kept telling me, but what was really behind it was he'd started to question his priorities and his life. He regretted giving up on his marriage and being away from his kids because of his job. He was wondering if it was all worth it, the same way I had been. I hoped I had saved him a little soul searching, but he was still going to have to decide for himself what to do. I hoped he'd call his wife and that she would give him a second chance. I wanted him to have the sense of stability and happiness Arly had given me. He was going to need it for what was coming. We *all* were.

Maybe I should have my own column, like Dear Abby. Really. Maybe that would be more fun than stripping anyway, which I was thinking of quitting again. Unless of course I caught Arly at another strip joint, then I'd dance all over his ass.

Anyway. I had other things to worry about right now. Like old TV shows. I had come to the conclusion whatever or whoever was trying to reach me, ghost or ghoul, had picked *Mister Ed* as an in-joke, knowing I would eventually stumble upon the played backwards Satanic messages connection because I had with Praetallious. Which might mean whatever was trying to reach me was another of those things that had escaped when Arly lopped off Ficatier's noggin. Who'da thunk that cute theme song would be a vessel for Evil? Bet Wilbur never saw *that* coming.

However, I was ready to file *Mister Ed* for the moment, but that other show, *Sliver of Darkness*…something about that and the fact the actor had mysteriously disappeared played hell with my intuition—I liked to call it my "stripper sense", because it was the same doom-filled feeling I had experienced the night that girlfriend killer came into the Lagoon. That show popping up on the old TV and everything going black and white had happened for a specific reason. But what was it? I guessed it had something to do with Brant Lamont, so I was going to need to do some research on our missing actor when I got home.

But was it him trying to contact me or something else masquerading as him, using pieces of that man's life to lure me into trouble I might not be lucky enough to get out of this time? Last time I was saved by a frickin' monkey. That doesn't happen everyday. Assuming for the moment it was Lamont, what did he want? That would mean he hadn't just disappeared; it meant he was dead. And maybe had gone to Hell and escaped, which was not comforting in the least.

A sound from my radio pulled me from my thoughts. A kind of crackling snap of a sound. I glanced at the radio. It wasn't on so it shouldn't have been making any noise period. I'd recently had satellite installed, though. Maybe there was something wrong with it.

As I came to a stop light, I reached out and pressed the radio button. I had it set on the local news station.

...struck again last night near the waterfront. The killer, who the papers have named the New Salem Ripper, left the mutilated body of Angela Delario, a prostitute, in an alley near Gibson's Antiques. A homeless man discovered the corpse slightly past 4 a.m. The torso had been ripped throat to pubis, a number of the organs cut free and scattered about the body...

Oh, swell. As if New Salem didn't have enough Evil floating through the Hell Door we had to have a serial whacko running around imitating Jack the Ripper. The thought of it made me a little jittery, because I generally got out of the Lagoon in the early morning hours, just about the time this guy liked to strike. Maybe I should have Pete start walking me—

Oh, *ca-rap.*

And I do mean crap. Because suddenly the local news changed and all the color disappeared from my world again.

SEVEN

Color My Rainbow in Noir

...In other news, police still have no new leads in the disappearance of New Salem's own Brant Lamont, who vanished last week after a performance of Sliver of Darkness *at the New Salem Theater. Investigators appear stumped after questioning his co-star and rumored paramour, Lillian Marlene, the last person to see the esteemed thespian the night of his disappearance. Lamont began his career in movies and was once being groomed as the next Clark Gable until a dispute with a studio head relegated him to bit parts and a pilot television series. His summer replacement show,* Sliver of Darkness, *lasted a brief six episodes before cancellation, but the show has been enjoying success locally as a theater production...*

What the hell? Not only had my world turned into a gray-screen panorama but my radio had jumped backwards over forty years. And this time there was no mistaking what or who the message was about. Brant Lamont, the probably late and maybe even lamented vanished actor.

Horns blaring made me notice the light had turned green. At least I think it was green; it was hard to tell in black and white. I stepped on the gas and immediately noticed something wrong with the pedal. It was much higher, thicker. The steering wheel in my hands felt thick, too, larger than the Beretta's, and the dashboard held none of the usual LED indicators. It was all dials and needles. A metallic plate on the dash said: American Motors. Rambler.

Rambler? I remember my father telling me my grandfather had one of those, a big blue and white one.

I peered through the window, noticing all the cars around me were larger, maybe late '50s' models.

Shaken, I spotted a parking space on the side of the road and pulled over to the curb. The car maneuvered like a truck and it took some muscle to actually turn the steering wheel. When I hit the brake pedal nothing really happened until I practically stood on it. Damn, I forgot cars didn't used to have power steering and brakes. People must have been stronger in the '60s.

My heart started to pound. I couldn't help it. Everything around me felt cold and it dawned on me my hands were encased in long black gloves. I glanced at the rearview mirror and nearly freaked.

Crap on a cracker, I was dressed like Jackie Kennedy! A kerchief? You had to be kidding me. My hair was in some kind of French pleat, which was scary enough, but I was wearing a waist-length jacket with decorative pockets and raised seams and my backpack had turned into some kind of ugly large handbag. What I was wearing wasn't even a stripping costume. I don't think. I tugged at the arms of the coat. Nope, they weren't pull-away. Definitely not a stripping outfit. It was the real deal. Whatever had thrust me back into a black and white '60s world had been kind enough to consider my wardrobe. Yipee.

A song suddenly started chiming from the radio, jerking me from the shock caused by my attire. It was a jaunty yet strangely haunting song with harpsichords and high voices, but no words. It transfixed me for a moment and I just knew I was not going to be able to get it out of my head for weeks.

As the song continued, my gaze drifted back to the street. People strolled by, all dressed in fashions at least forty years out of date. No one so much as glanced at my car or me and I wondered if they even saw me. Was I invisible to them? Merely observing the past and not really part of it? Maybe the horns had been blaring at someone else.

I grabbed the handle and shoved open the door, which took a lot more strength than I expected it to. What the hell did they used to make car doors out of, anyway?

I got out, and damn near fell flat on my face. Looking down I saw the reason: heels. I was in black pumps with heels instead of the toe-less flats I had slipped on before leaving the house this morning. Not that I wasn't used to walking in heels. I used stiletto heels in my dance routines sometimes. I just hadn't been quite prepared for them. I was also in a skirt that fell well below my knees and hugged my thighs a little tighter than it should have, making walking even more awkward.

As I stood by the car, movement roughly fifty yards down the sidewalk drew my attention from my dress mode. A man. A strange man wearing a dark suit and a flowing black cape drifted towards me, seeming to float more than actually walk. An air of...what? Sadness? Depression? somehow emanated from him like a black fog; it swept over me in a dark wave, seeped into my being.

"Hey!" I shouted at the man in the dark suit. "Hey you!" At first he made no sign that he'd even heard me, then he paused and turned towards me, but his face...

Despite the daylight, shadows beneath a large drooping hat completely obscured his features. The cape's turned up collar concealed his lower face. But it wasn't just shadows, was it? It was a dark blur of some sort, as if his features were out of focus. A laugh suddenly whispered from unseen lips and he glided forward again.

"Wait!" I yelled, impulsiveness overcoming the fear twisting in my stomach. I tried to run after him but couldn't move fast enough, not just because of the heels or the tight skirt, but because I felt as if I were trapped in a dream, the kind where you run with all your might but the air is made out of molasses and your limbs are made out of lead.

Yet while I moved in slow-motion, the man moved at regular speed, quickly out-distancing me. In the background the song still chimed from the car radio. I thought I caught a name as it ended. Welk. Lawrence Welk Orchestra...

Ok, now that was really disturbing. I had memories of my parents watching that every Saturday night. My dad use to make a big pan of popcorn with real butter and sit Pat and I in front of the TV with him and my mom. I have vague recollections of a Halloween and Christmas show, and an old guy with a German accent and some dancers or something. And bubbles. Lots of bubbles.

But there were no bubbles here and nothing about the experience felt warm and friendly.

Then, suddenly, the black and white '60s world vanished. Color, heat, modern clothing and cars returned in a blink. A handful of people on the sidewalk gawked at me.

I should have known better, but I asked anyway. "Did any of you..." Ok, how was I going to put this and not sound like a complete loon? I couldn't see any rational way. "Was everything black and white a minute ago? Did you see the old cars?"

The stares went from wonderment to mild fear and people started walking away from me. Fast.

"Just great," I muttered, knowing it would be useless to go after them. They hadn't experienced what I had and that was just peachy, wasn't it? It was bad enough being a nut in a whole can of them but being the lone nut?

My own clothing had returned to normal; so had my Beretta. My heart on the other hand was still doing an Irish jig. I wondered if maybe I hadn't given Johnny the wrong advice. Maybe it would be better to run, because how many times could you experience something that completely turned your world upside down before you went crazy?

I had the feeling I was close to finding out.

EIGHT

A Little Less Contemplation, a Little More Traction

My hands were cemented to the steering wheel and I still had the urge to shudder by the time I pulled into the parking lot of my town-house complex, Captain's Landing. I drove past the sign shaped like a ship's wheel and the rusty old anchor in the yard, wondering if I was going to pee my pants from all the coffee keeping me awake and the fear ping-ponging around in my stomach.

No one else on the street had noticed the world shifting to black and white. They hadn't seen the '60s' cars and clothing. The more I thought about it the more I wondered if maybe it wasn't the supernatural. Maybe I was just experiencing some kind of nervous breakdown.

But it was a strange breakdown. I had never heard of *Sliver of Darkness* before last night and I couldn't have told you much about '60s' cars and clothing had my life depended on it. I suppose there was a chance I could have subconsciously absorbed the information some-where, maybe as a kid from pictures, and maybe I just didn't remem-ber hearing that song or seeing the TV show…Ok, so maybe I couldn't dismiss the nervous breakdown theory quite yet.

Wait. Puddin' Head had seen everything turn black and white last night. He had awoken grumbling about the cold.

Hadn't he? Maybe I just assumed that was what he had been grum-bling about. He grumbled about everything. Maybe he was just sore about being woken up.

I suddenly didn't feel any better about the nervous breakdown the-ory because the more I thought about it the more I realized I was bas-ing my grip on reality on the fact a cat might have experienced the same phenomena I had. And I couldn't exactly ask him about it. Well, I could ask, but getting a coherent answer was problematic.

I pulled into my parking space and turned the ignition switch to auxiliary. My hand shook as I reached for the radio button. The radio came on, but it was the news station I normally had it tuned to. I jabbed it off, feeling no better.

Evil's trying to shake you up, I told myself, make you think you're nuts. Hadn't I seen too much weird crap since the Sisters of the Snake to doubt what had happened or my sanity?

Maybe. Or maybe everything was getting to me. I was still upset over being close to a lead on my sister a couple weeks back and seeing what might have been her ghost, then having that lead and the ghost evaporate and leave me with little more than I had in the first place.

Dammit, I missed her and needed to find out the truth. I didn't need this supernatural crap getting in the way right now.

I thumped the steering wheel with the heel of my hands a let out a curse because it hurt. You think I would have learned from the last time I hit it not to do that.

You'd think I would have learned a lot of things, but maybe I'm just one of those people who have to be hit over the head with a hammer before they figure crap out.

Or get sacrificed to a demon.

I shuddered, sighed and grabbed my backpack. I rummaged through the front pouch for my cell phone and pulled it out. After flipping open the cover I hit the button for Sturdevant's cell. It rang twice before he picked up and he was already groaning. I put it on speaker and tossed the cell on the car seat. They say the phones give you brain cancer so I was keeping it way from my head as much as possible. Yes, I am blonde. So what?

"Chlo, didn't you just leave me?" came his voice. "Please don't tell me—"

"That's what I'm going to tell you, Johnny, so you might as well give me your biggest sigh now."

He did. I swore it scared birds out of a nearly by tree. "What is it?" he asked at last.

"It happened again."

"The black and white thing?"

"Yeah, that. And more. This time I saw old cars from the '60s and some guy in a black suit and cape with a shadowy face. He laughed at me."

"Laughed at you? What kind of laugh?"

"Whispery type, creepy. You know the drill. I yelled to him and he ignored me, just kept walking. I'm almost sure it was that Lamont guy you told me about."

"Lamont's dead in all likelihood, and even if he was to just suddenly show up on a street corner he'd be what? 70? 80?"

"But this street corner was back in the 1960s. He'd be younger."

"You said you couldn't see his face."

"But his laugh sounded just like the one on that TV show and the way he was dressed..."

"Chlo..." Exasperation. Mixed with a little worry. He managed to get that all into one syllable of my name. Arly did that sometimes. I was starting to get a complex.

"I'm almost certain it was him, Johnny."

"Ok, say it was. What did he want? Why did he just walk away?"

"I don't know!" My voice went up a little. "Evil never dials direct, you know that."

"But there had to be some reason, right? Some clue?"

I thought about it a moment. "There was a song..."

"Not the *Mister Ed* theme, please tell me."

"No, not this time. It went, la la la la la la..."

"That doesn't help."

"Carrying a tune isn't my strong suit. Only dancing to them. But I think I heard something about Lawrence Welk."

"Lawrence Welk? You're right, it was an old ghost and this just got a lot scarier."

"Very funny says the guy in the *Mister Ed* Fanclub."

That shut him up.

"Check the nursing homes. Welk was a bit before my time and I was always more a Zombies kind of guy if I have to listen to '60s music."

"That's not even funny," I said. "Zombies and I don't mix."

"I'm aware. But I got nothing. I'll see what I can find on Lamont, like I said, but don't hold your breath."

"I heard...uh, something on the news about his disappearance."

"What? There's been no new—"

"Wasn't new. Was old. '60s old news. Coming over my car radio."

"This is just getting worse by the minute."

"Doesn't it always?" I said it with a slight chuckle in my voice but I really didn't see any humor in it.

"The one constant since you and Arlo started with that whole Czcarabus business last year."

"The report said something about his leading lady being the last to see him."

"Lillian something or other, I think."

"Lillian Marlene."

"That's it. Lamont was married, but it was common knowledge he and Marlene had a thing going."

"Under the lamplight?"

"What?"

"Nevermind, Bad joke."

"Uh-huh. How do you even know that song?"

"Did a WW2 routine to it once, long time ago."

"I can't imagine."

"And you probably shouldn't. You don't think maybe his wife found out about them and toasted his naughty bits, do you?"

"Like I said, from what I recall it was common knowledge, so she most likely knew. Plus there were rumors he was homosexual and trying to cover it up. But I can't tell you for certain because I know damn little about that case. Look it up on the Internet; there's a—"

"Fanclub, yeah, I know." I reached over and snapped the phone shut, then tucked it into the backpack. After zipping the pouch shut, I grabbed the backpack and climbed out of the car. I don't have to tell you frustration was driving me as crazy as the nerves fluttering in my gut. I wished Arly was back. He was the detective. He was so much better at tracking down leads than I was and frankly after Praetallious I could use the vacation.

I headed for my apartment, #12, letting my keys dangle in my hand, a little anxious the whole world might go black and white again. But it didn't. Instead I got something even more worrisome.

Because when I opened my door and looked into my living room something was sitting on the coffee table. Something that damn well didn't belong there.

NINE

Hey Hey with the Monkey

"Can't she just pick up a damned phone?" I said as I banged the door shut and stood looking at the furry little reprobate sitting on my coffee table. "You're lucky Puddin' Head's too lazy to get his big fluffy ass down here. He's territorial."

I was getting over the initial shock of discovering Bob in my apartment, which meant I was blabbering while trying to get my heart to stop slamming against my ribcage. My gaze lifted to the slider door, which was ajar and I realized I had forgotten to put the pipe back in the track last night. I was pretty certain, though, that I had locked it, but that didn't seem to matter much where Genie Lansing and her little smelly cohort were concerned.

Yes, I said Bob. Bob the monkey. Bob the supposedly 600-year-old dead monkey, midget confident of one M-S Genie Lansing, museum curator and all around enigma. The last time Bob showed up in my apartment he'd left behind a locket belonging to my sister, one I had used to destroy the demon, Praetallious.

Bob was doing the crinkly monkey forehead thing and making weird monkey movements with his mouth.

"What do you want?" I asked him, like he was really going to answer but what do you say to a monkey you come home to find sitting on your coffee table—"So are you a Planet of the Apes fan?"

I tossed my jean backpack onto the dining room table, then took the three steps down into the sunken living room. Bob just looked at me and I hoped he wasn't getting any ideas about flinging poop. I've told you monkeys are good at that sort of thing. But did dead monkeys poop?

He's not dead, a voice of reason in my mind tried to assure me. He couldn't be. No frickin' way.

But you saw his bones in a box, a second voice rebutted. And you know what goes on in this town.

Guess which voice was winning? There was something damned strange about Genie Lansing and that extended to her pet. And as I was always telling Johnny, this was New Salem. Weirder things had happened. Weirder things had shown up at my apartment, for cryin' out loud.

But I did sort of owe the little putz my life.

Then I noticed Bob had something clutched in his creepy little monkey hand.

"Oh, you've got to be kiddin' me. Not again."

Bob made a noise I would have sworn was a laugh. He set the object on the table with a dull tap and chittered. That's right, he chittered. Then skittered. He jumped off the table and loped to the slider door. He looked back once with an expression that was somehow almost human and might have broadcast a sarcastic, "Good luck", then darted through the slider opening.

I ran to the door, closed it. After locating the pipe, I jammed it in the track and let out a small shiver. I was no longer afraid of Bob but something about finding a monkey in your apartment...

I've told you I had this problem with monkeys stemming from that poop-flinging incident with my sister? Well, that wasn't my only bad experience with the little turds. My parents had taken Pat and me to the Shine Circus—I think we were maybe five, but don't quote me on that. They had these chimps. Now, chimps are pretty large when you are five. And they suffer from chimpy body odor. Pat and I were in the front row when a clown—like clowns aren't frickin' scary enough—lost control of his chimp and the damn thing ended up in my lap. I remember being terrified and shrieking but the audience was laughing. Pat was laughing.

The chimp didn't do anything particular except startle me and smell like a chimp. But that hadn't mattered to a frightened five-year-old who had evil chimp nightmares for the next few weeks. Pat, being Pat, got a big kick out of it. I remember shortly before Halloween that year she'd gotten one of those gorilla masks. She'd never ceased to miss a chance to hide in the darkened hallway of our house and scare the living hell out of me by jumping out of the linen closet. I had done some screaming on that, let me tell you. It had taken my parents a half hour to get me to stop screaming.

So monkeys for me were a bad omen and this case was apparently proving to be no exception.

It was happening again. Whatever this ghost—or whatever it was—of Brant Lamont wanted it appeared tied in with something that had escaped from when Arly disposed of Angelique Ficatier. It had to be related, didn't it? Otherwise Lansing wouldn't have sent Bob to my apartment. Beware of monkeys bearing gifts. What was this one for? To protect me? Or possibly to get me killed?

I got no chance to think of an answer because my cell phone rang in my backpack and I let out one of those idiotic chirps of fear.

TEN

The Girl from Yesterday

I hadn't heard from Amanda Connors in probably three years, so getting her call came as a surprise to say the least. And of course getting it directly on the heels of monkey feet running out of my townhouse was just poor timing for my already over-strung nerves.

But maybe I needed the diversion from things supernatural and black and white. So after the usual "What have you been up to?" and "I'm so surprised to hear from you," chit chat I had agreed to meet her at a coffee shop on the waterfront near the Red Lagoon. I'd heard something in her voice, melancholy maybe, so I felt a little obligated.

Amanda and I had worked together on the circuit for a brief time. She was probably a year younger than I was, without a lot of natural dancing talent but enough front porch and length of leg to make up for it. Most guys weren't looking to be a judge on *Dancing with the Stars* when it came to girls getting naked anyway.

I remember her being quiet, and we'd never really connected, so I wasn't sure why she should look me up now. But, for that matter, she hadn't really connected with any of the girls. She'd kept mostly to herself and after her shifts she'd never hung out with any of the other dancers. What she did in her off time was anybody's guess and one day she'd just not shown up for work. That was the last I had seen of her.

The Coffee Shoppe—yeah, that's what it was called, real original, huh?—was one of those dark gloomy places tucked between old brick buildings that the college crowd liked to hang out in with their lattés and laptops. The walls were of dark brick, the lights subdued to the point of tripping over tables and a blend of cloying spice smells saturated the air along with the scent of coffee. I am not a big fan of Chai, incidentally. A row of tables and drab two-seat couches lined one wall and a coffee counter the opposite one. Construction paper posters with bad artwork advertised various musical performers scheduled to cram their brand of noise down patrons' throats every Friday and Saturday night.

I stopped at the counter and ordered a black decaf, like I hadn't peed enough today. I spotted Amanda sitting at a back table, her head slightly down, as if lost in thought. Her auburn hair hugged her soft features and she still had the biggest brown eyes and a matching bra size. As I approached her table she looked up, and I noticed sadness in those eyes, but she quickly hid it with joy over seeing me.

I set my coffee on the table and she stood, gave me a hug. A chill went through me. Although it was a warm day she felt cold and I noticed her face was a bit pale. Maybe she was coming down with something.

"It's been ages, Chloe," she said, sitting again.

I slipped my jean backpack off my shoulder and set it on a spare seat, then sat myself.

"I was surprised to get your call." I tried taking a sip of my coffee but it was hot enough to boil lobster. "Surprised you were able to get my cell number, too."

She offered a soft smile. "I called the Lagoon. A man there gave it to me. I couldn't find your landline."

I nodded. "I had it changed and unlisted after…some issues last December."

"Stalker boyfriend?" She laughed an easy laugh.

No, zombies and witches, I wanted to say, but refrained. "So what brings you to New Salem?"

"My great aunt."

My brow cinched. "You have relatives here? I thought you were from New York originally."

"I am. My family was, but my aunt was always drawn to New Salem…maybe it was the sea air, who knows? She spent a lot of time here, bought an old cottage house in the '60s."

I nodded. I was a bit surprised anybody would be drawn here, given the town's history and happenings. I figured they'd be leaving in droves soon if things kept up. "So you're just visiting her?"

The sadness washed back into her eyes and she frowned. "For the last time, I guess."

My belly tightened a little. "That doesn't sound very good."

She shook her head. "It isn't. She had a stroke, ended up confined to a wheelchair. Can't talk, can't do much of anything but sit and stare. She's in Willow Pines. I…got a call from them saying they can barely make her eat anymore and there probably isn't a lot of time left."

I placed my hand over hers, squeezed. "I'm so sorry, Amanda. If I can help in any way…"

She gave me a thin smile. "Well, maybe you can. I need a job while I'm here, so if you could maybe get me into the Lagoon, just…well just until…"

I nodded, pulled my hand back. Man, her hand was ice cold, but now I attributed it to worry over her aunt. That probably explained why she had no coffee, too; her nerves were jangled enough already. "I can talk to Pete, but I have to be honest, it's a bad time to have a night job in New Salem…"

Her left eyebrow arched and a puzzled look came into her eyes. "You say that like something awful's happening in this town."

I sighed, not wanting to go into the details of supernatural boos escaping from Hell. "There's some kind of serial killer in town. Another girl was murdered last night on the waterfront."

"Serial killer?" She looked as if she were about to change her mind about staying in New Salem and I couldn't blame her.

"It's been going on for a few weeks, now. I think there's been three or four killings so far."

"Jesus, in a little town like this?"

"You'd be surprised what goes on in this town." My tone carried way more sarcasm than I intended.

She gave me another puzzled look but I didn't elaborate. Instead, I finally took a sip of my own coffee, which was just down to paint-melting temperature.

"I don't have much choice but to stay…at least for a little while."

I nodded, unzipped a pouch on my backpack and pulled out my cell. I punched the button for the Lagoon and waited for Pete to pick up.

I got his usual grumble. He sounded a lot like my cat.

"I'm sending a girl over to you, Pete," I said ignoring his attitude. He was always pissy this time of the day. "Her name's Amanda."

Pete grumbled a question and I automatically glanced at Amanda's rack. "Oh, they're big enough..."

Amanda laughed as I hung up.

"Men never change," she said.

"Good thing they don't or we'd be working at Wal-Mart and they're not fond of topless cashiers."

"Maybe it would improve customer relations."

I nodded. "Well, at least half of them anyway..."

"Thanks, Chloe. I appreciate it. I know we didn't really know each other very well, but I remembered you mentioning this town and I could really use...a friend while I am here." Sadness burrowed deep into her voice again.

"You ok, Amanda? You got a place to stay? You can always sleep on my couch." I knew it was a bad idea offering her that, considering my little trouble with black and white ghosts and invading capuchins, but I felt bad for her. I wanted to help in some way. I hate seeing people sad.

"I'm good. Staying at my great aunt's old cottage. Going to have to get it ready to sell anyway." She stood and I shoved my phone back into the pouch and zipped it.

Standing, I gave her another hug. "Go see Pete."

"My next stop," she said, offering a fragile smile. I watched her walk out of the shop, noting no confidence in her stride. Something about the way she carried herself reminded me of a lost little girl. Her aunt's condition must have been really wearing on her, but I couldn't help thinking there was more to her melancholic demeanor than she had let on.

ELEVEN

Interlude

I couldn't stop thinking about how sad Amanda had looked at the Coffee Shoppe. I know dealing with your great aunt dying wasn't easy but the more I thought about it the more I became convinced there was something she wasn't telling me. I knew her in passing, but didn't *know* her well enough to go prying into her business.

The weird thing was, my gut was telling me for whatever other reason she'd come to New Salem that reason somehow tied into me. My "stripper sense" kicking in again. I didn't like coincidences and that she had suddenly shown up and contacted me on the tail of strange occurrences plaguing my life again…well, maybe it *was* just a coincidence, but the way things went in New Salem I couldn't help reading more into it.

You're being paranoid, now, I assured myself. All this Evil hooey had me jumping at shadows and grasping at connections where none existed.

I could remember telling myself that before. Too many times to count, in fact. And you know how that went. I nearly ended up with the plague a couple weeks ago.

After I pulled into my townhouse parking space, I sat in the car another few minutes, trying to figure out a possible link, but came up empty. Maybe when I saw her at the Lagoon I could talk her into going to the diner after work for coffee and see if I could get closer to her. Even if her appearance didn't somehow connect to me, something else was going on with her and maybe she needed a friend to help her through it.

Speaking of the Lagoon...I fished my cell out of my backpack and gave Pete a call, to see whether Amanda had really gone there for a job.

"She came and went," Pete said, his voice blaring from the cell speaker. "I gave her the gig. She starts tomorrow. Nice set on that one."

I laughed. "Delicate, Pete." But tomorrow was good, since this was my day off and I needed to spend some time working on a costume. No, nothing from the '60s. Pete wanted a Disco theme, so it was spangles all the way. I'm pretty sure the guys didn't care what I was wearing as long as I wasn't wearing it for long.

"What can I say? That's why I hired *you*."

"And I thought all this time it was for my bubbly personality and brains." Something hit me, then, something Amanda had said at the Coffee Shoppe. "Hey, Pete, do me a favor and don't give my cell number out to anyone who calls, ok? It's private. It was ok this time because I know Amanda, but with the trouble Arly and I have been having..."

A grunt came from the cell. "I know better than that, Chlo. I didn't give it to anyone."

What? But Amanda had told me...

"You didn't give it to Amanda when she asked you for it?"

"No one but you has called here today. It's too early. I let her in because she was a friend of yours, but I never gave her your number."

After signing off with Pete, I sat there a moment, puzzled. How would she have gotten my cell number otherwise and why had she told me Pete had given it to her? I supposed it didn't matter really, because she had it and she was a friend, but I didn't like people lying to me.

After a few moments, I let it go, then tried calling Lansing again, knowing it was likely a lost cause. I had some questions for her about her reprobate monkey getting into my living room and leaving another trinket. Her punky receptionist informed me Lansing wasn't in and no, she had no idea when she would be back. No surprise there. Why that woman couldn't just be upfront...it made me start to wonder about her again, about just which side was she on. Evil? Good?

This time I got another answer: her own. Maybe she was working to her own ends and they were good or evil depending on the circumstances.

Who or what exactly was Lansing, anyway? Was she even human? Was Bob? She said Bob was 600 years old. How old did that make her? Why had fire bothered her so irrationally? How did she seem to get into and out of rooms without exits so mysteriously? How did she know some of the things she knew? Including something about my sister she was forbidden, or some such nonsense, to tell me?

The more I dwelled on the woman the more questions I had.

She did give Arly the sword, I reminded myself, the one that had taken down Angelique Ficatier. Well, Ficatier might not really be totally taken down, another voice countered. I had glimpsed her in Praetallious' eyes.

Which meant what?

Maybe nothing. It might mean Lansing had told the truth or it might mean Lansing had concocted some sort of elaborate plan to her own end.

You're really getting paranoid, now, I told myself.

Funny thing is, getting kicked in the ass by the supernatural will do that to you.

I stuffed my cell into my backpack and got out of the car. I noted it was past Puddin' Head's lunchtime and if you think Evil was a bitch you should see His Majesty when he doesn't eat on time.

TWELVE

A One, A Two, A Thank Ya, Boys...

If anyone had told me I would someday be on the Internet research-ing Lawrence Welk I would have laughed. Really loud. But a little af-ter six in the evening here I was, sitting at my desk with yet another cup of coffee, ignoring a ticked off cat and running a Cloogle search for the conductor's greatest hits. All I needed was champagne bubbles floating around my bedroom.

Puddin' Head's whiskers were in a bunch, which was nothing un-usual for him, but apparently he objected to me moving his living room pillow while I had done some sewing on a costume. He'd have to get over it, but I wondered why I had gotten attached to a cat with the personality of an old man with uncomfortable dentures. It probably said more about me than him, so I wasn't going to probe too deeply to figure out exactly what it was.

Anyhoo, the search didn't take anywhere near as long as I thought it would. I had a tune without a title and figured in Welk's career I'd have to search through hundreds of songs and didn't even know if this one might be a cut from some obscure album. I lucked out because it came up immediately and turned out to be his biggest hit. It helped that I typed 1961 into the search box along with his name.

I discovered a VidTube page with the video of a spinning .45 re-cord. The song's title was *Calcutta*, and from the first note I knew it was the same haunting harpsichord song that had come out of my car radio. Listening to it, I got the weirdest sensation of being whisked back in time, and that made me nervous. Was the room suddenly going to turn black and white again? That sure as hell wouldn't improve Puddin' Head's mood any. But for the moment that didn't happen.

The song ended and I just stared at the page. I now knew what the song was. I knew its chart placements and the date, 1961, same as *Sliver of Darkness* and Lamont's disappearance. The thing I didn't know was why it had been coming out of my car radio earlier today and what it had to do with the ghost of a vanished actor.

Maybe it had nothing to do with Lamont, like the *Mister Ed* snippet on the TV. But then again the *Mister Ed* theme song played backwards had an urban legend attached to it about Satanic messages. I wondered if this song had the same sort of association, if it was some sort of clue or warning...

I ran another search for *Calcutta* and any related legends and that took me a good hour of sifting through a hundred useless webpages, too many of them filled with naked people from a play that went by nearly the same name.

After fifteen minutes of that I was fidgeting in my chair; after a half hour I was chewing off a nail and by the end of the hour I was thoroughly frustrated and had basically squat. Zip. Nada. No freakin' urban legends were associated with that song that I could find. So why had it played? Was it just a coincidence after the newscast about Lamont Brant's disappearance?

I tended to doubt it. The Bads worked in mysterious ways and I figured I was missing some link. I spent another fifteen minutes searching, but came up empty.

I blew out a long sigh, which annoyed the cat enough to jump off the end of the bed and harrumph out of the room.

"You can be neutered..." I yelled after him, but he ignored me the way he usually does.

I went back to Cloogle and typed in Brant Lamont's name. Sure enough, a fanclub, just like Johnny had told me.

When I brought up the page I saw two pictures, both set against a mysterious smoky blue-black background. An audio file started playing, and the same eerie laugh I'd heard on the TV show shuddered out of my computer speakers, then:

Who knows what crimes cripple the minds of the guilty?

I clicked off my volume button. I really didn't need to listen to that again after last night's little episode.

The first photo consisted of the actor wearing a slouch hat and black cape, forearm raised across his lower face. All that showed were piercing brown eyes and a slightly hooked nose.

The second picture was of the actor himself, in his younger movie days, I guessed, with slicked back hair, and angular features. His nose didn't detract from his overall handsomeness. He reminded me a bit of a young Orson Welles, before he got as big as a house. I could see why women would have gone for him in his time, and maybe even a few men, if what Johnny had said about the homosexual rumors were true.

There were a number of related page links and I went through each. Most spewed the usual Hollywood-hyped bio garbage, though one did focus on what friends called the actor's "dark" personality. Apparently after his movie career ended he'd been known to drink and lash out violently at friends, and fall into deep depressions that lasted weeks at a time. He wasn't particularly depressed over the short-lived TV gig, however, considering himself above such pulp entertainment. One article from a magazine at the time quoted him making no bones about being glad the show had been cancelled.

Which didn't really explain why, if he hated it so, he had taken the part in the play. Or maybe it did. Ego. He was an actor and a play was a step above a TV series to a man who thought himself a trained thespian.

Of course, I was assigning my own assumptions to a man I didn't really know, but I bet I wasn't far off the mark.

Another page showed a photo of his ingénue, Lillian Marlene. She was a good twenty years his junior, with looks that somewhat resembled Marilyn Monroe, but harder, with a sharper chin and cheekbones, and darker hair. Little was written about their liaison, but it did mention Lamont was married at the time and the affair wasn't a big secret. In those days studio heads protected their own and their own's image, but since Lamont was on the outs word had leaked out quick. Marlene was an up and comer and probably thought she had something to gain by clinging to an older actor, even a somewhat deposed one, and of course what he had to gain was obvious.

I discovered his wife had died a couple of years after his disappearance and was buried in a local cemetery, so talking to her was out of the question…well, at least I hoped it was, but in New Salem…

I couldn't find anything much about Marlene and what had become of her. The fansite ignored her for the most part, almost showing disdain in their summery of her part in Lamont's life.

Hero worship is a weird thing. We mere mortals hold them up to higher standards and anyone not deserving of being a part of that standard ends up dismissed. This site catered to Lamont as if he were some cult hero and Lillian Marlene tainted that image, so she merely got a passing mention.

I uttered a small laugh. I understood in a way. I recalled my father and mother taking me and Patricia to a local TV show when we were a little past six years old. It was a show for kids, where a young woman invited locals to participate in an episode and play games like Reach for the Moon, Stomper Clompers and sing songs for a half hour. My father somehow got us on the show and I can't even tell you how excited Pat and I were about it. It was one of those experiences as a child you were never supposed to forget.

I never forgot it, all right, but for a reason my father and mother probably would have preferred to avoid.

The show had this clown. Ok, I know what you're thinking: clowns are never good. They're basically just evil stuffed into a funny suit. I kind of agree, but this clown was my hero at the time. At least until after all the kids were taken backstage to meet some of the behind-the-scenes crew.

This particular clown was named Mr. Buggles. Yeah, I know. Don't laugh. I was six, remember? Apparently Mr. Buggles had a thing for the young woman hosting the show and for every other young thing in a skirt. Pat and I wandered away from the group tour backstage—ok, you know that was Pat's fault, right? She was always daring me to do things I shouldn't and this was no different. My parents should have known better than to leave us alone with the tour guides, given Pat's history of getting into trouble and blaming me for it. But, anyway, Mr. Buggles wasn't the honkingest clown in the horn box because he had left his dressing room door partially open and guess who was in the room with him?

You got it, Miss Maples, the show's perky play guide. Now, at six neither Pat nor I realized quite what Mr. Buggles was doing on top of her, but let me tell you the sight of a naked clown ass is something I hope I never see again.

Mr. Buggles went from hero to creepy in an instant in my book. Pat started laughing hysterically and of course they heard us. Mr. Buggles yelled things no kid should hear come out of a clown and tried chasing us, his pants down around his knees. Miss Maples came right behind him, her skirt way too far south of her border. I got to see things I really didn't need to see at that age and Pat kept pointing and laughing at his dangling parts as I tried to drag her down the hallway and back to the group.

It didn't much matter because the group had heard Mr. Buggles' blue streak and when they came around the corner to see a pantsless clown swearing at and chasing two six-year-olds…well, Mr. Buggles was never on another episode and Miss Maples wound up replaced as show hostess a short time later.

I never watched that show again. I think Pat might have, but she found the incident a whole lot funnier than I did. My parents weren't real happy with what happened, either, and Mr. Buggles is lucky no one pressed charges.

Like I said, heroes are a funny thing. Easily built up and sometimes as easily torn down, but this page still glamorized Brant Lamont, philanderer or not.

I read through more of the stuff, locating a page that contained a number of articles from the local newspaper at the time of his disappearance. Most reported he was last seen with Marlene. Apparently they were commonly noticed on the beach or hanging around the theater after the patrons left. She claimed they had just stayed after-hours to discuss some line changes for the next night's performance. Yeah, I bet. When police questioned her she had told them they had simply run through lines, then gone their separate ways.

That, as they say, was that.

Except it wasn't, was it? He had vanished without a trace. With no discernable motive.

I wondered if, given his temperament, maybe Marlene had broken it off with him that night and perhaps he hadn't taken the news well. Maybe even bad enough to kill himself. In that case, in New Salem, there were more places to do yourself in and make sure your body was never found than you could shake an Inquisition sword at. The beaches were littered with sea caves and the woods at the edge of town went on forever.

Had he offed himself?

Then another question suddenly nagged at me. Had Evil taken a hand in his vanishing?

Is that why his ghost was coming back now?

Maybe I was grasping at straws, but in New Salem, who knew?

THIRTEEN

Sister Snake Act

I was walking naked through the night. Snow crunched beneath my feet and a winter wind caressed my nude body like chilled velvet. Darkly erotic, the sensation made my belly tingle deep within and my breasts ache with wanton desire that only came with...

Evil.

Flakes of snow drifted around me like tiny frozen skulls. They stung slightly as they touched my flesh, melted. Everything inside me wanted to stop walking, turn, flee, but some force compelled me to keep moving forward. Whispers reached my ears, hungry whispers, craving whispers, ubiquitous and menacing.

Feelings inside me intensified, great waves of lust, desire, of black passion surging, swelling, becoming overwhelming. My nipples distended, throbbing.

What is this? What was happening to me?

Ahead, a stand of leafless trees loomed like blackened skeletons, their branches reaching with bony ebony fingers, as if clutching for me, as if grasping for the life-force within my warm body, wanting to wrench it free, devour it.

Beyond the skeletal shapes lay the looming bulk of a great mansion.

No! I wanted to scream, recognizing it, though I had not been part of the final conflict within its cursed walls, within that devil room that had nearly witnessed the rebirth of the demon Czcarabus. The Mayoral Mansion, where Angelique Ficatier had sought to bring Evil into this realm, where acts of depravity and lust had been committed by Milicent Creed and the Sisters of the Snake.

"This isn't possible!" I screamed. "I wasn't there!"

Within me the dark lust increased, sending shudders through my belly. With its force, my mouth came open in a soundless gasp, and for an instant I wanted to submit to it, let it envelop me, seep into every pore, every cell. I wanted to embrace every unspeakable desire I had never dared to imagine. I wanted to be taken by Evil, thrown to the snow and forced to surrender; I wanted it to penetrate my very soul.

You're a stripper, Chloe...you're no good...you're a toy for men, an object they lust over and us, then cast away...

"No!" I yelled at the dark whisper that filled the frigid air all about me. "I'm the one with the power, the one who controls them!"

A laugh, a woman's, reverberated through the frozen night air.

You are deluded, Everson. You are a sinner. You tell yourself you have power but you do not. They have it, all those men who watch you with their drunken lustful eyes, all those men who think of nothing but plunging their dirty—

"Liar! I know who you are! I know what you want!" I wrapped my arms across my breasts, with every remaining shred of my courage rebuking the voice.

The laugh shuddered out again, mocking me.

Do you? Do you really? You can't even begin to know. I will have him, Everson. I will have Grimm...

The trees thinned and I gazed upon the darkened hulk of the mansion. A great rumbling came from within its walls and the building trembled. Glass exploded from windows, mixing with falling snow and spiraling to the ground. Beams splintered, snapping with great *cracks* of sound. Stone crumbled and the house began to cave.

Two forms hurtled through a remaining upstairs window. Two men. I recognized them instantly: Arly and his son, David. They hit the ground, both stunned.

The Mayoral Mansion fell in upon itself, a great ball of blackness swallowing it as a hole opened beneath its foundations.

I stopped walking, stood rigid, frozen to the spot. I watched as Arly fell back into the snow, unconscious. But David, David remained awake. He struggled to push himself up to his hands and knees, and his gaze went to the collapsing structure.

Something arced from the mansion, as if Hell had regurgitated it; it hit the ground and rolled a half dozen yards. A round black object, it came to a stop a short ways from David, just as he reached his feet. He stared at it, shock welding onto his haggard face.

"Christ..." he whispered.

For an instant his gaze swung towards me but he gave no indication he saw I was standing there. As if he didn't see me. He bent, shoved his arms beneath Arly's and dragged him to a tree, then propped him against the trunk. Turning back to the object in the snow, he paused. Nodding slightly, he went to the object, grabbing it in his right hand. I could tell then he had grasped curls of ebony hair, because as he turned towards me again and began walking in my direction, and I could clearly see what the object was.

A head. A severed head.

Angelique Ficatier's head.

Waves of terror shuddered through me and I wanted to collapse but something inside, some stubborn glimmer of courage, wouldn't let me go down. He came forward, but I knew he wasn't truly seeing me; he was merely walking towards the long driveway to my right. He passed me, never acknowledging my presence, but the head in his hand...

Jesus! Its eyes were open, black and staring, glittering with anti-light, and I knew—*knew*—the thing saw me. A laugh ululated from its parted lips.

He will be mine... the thing whispered, the sound filling the air like a thousand snakes hissing and reverberating through every fiber of my being.

Her laugh crescendoed, saturating the night, but David didn't seem to hear it. He just kept walking, his features grim.

Then I woke up, screaming, in black and white.

FOURTEEN

Mr. Darkness

Everything in my room had gone colorless again. And cold. The scream died on my lips as I realized I had woken from one nightmare into another. I was still naked, having slept that way again since it was a warm night, and gooseflesh crawled across my skin.

The laugh followed me from the nightmare, shuddering through the room. But, no, it was different, not the same laugh, not Ficatier's. This laugh belonged to that character from the TV show. With it came a dark feeling of depression, from within and from without.

Moonlight sliced across the floor and bed and the curtain wafted under a cool breeze. I pressed my eyes closed, suddenly too freakin' afraid to even look around the room. With the laughing, came Puddin' Head's incessant snoring from the end of the bed and I almost let out a nervous giggle.

My heart started banging against my ribs and I seriously hoped I wasn't going to pee the bed. Note to self: Stop drinking coffee before going to sleep.

I forced open my eyes, stifling another scream that wanted to jump out of my mouth. I had faced the Sisters of the Snake and a zombie in my house, for chrissakes. I was brave. I was woman. I was stripper. I could confront anything or anyone.

I was lying. I was scared crapless.

The laugh echoed out again, almost a living thing, slithering in the shadowy room corners, writhing on the chilled air.

I grabbed the blanket and jerked it over my breasts. I had no desire to be ogled by any pervert ghost.

A figure stood in the corner of the room, emerging from the shadows as it if were somehow a part of them. Its shape was vaguely manlike, concealed beneath a flowing cape. Its features, bathed in ebony, were hidden by a slouch hat and an upturned collar.

"Who the hell are you?" I yelled at it, more out of sudden fear than bravery. I wanted to run, but there was nowhere to run and jumping out of bed naked didn't hold a hell of a lot of appeal, either, since the figure stood close to the door and I wasn't about to be leaping out of a second story window in my birthday suit. Most of the neighbors had no idea what I did for a living and seeing me running bare-assed through the middle of a moonlit night wasn't the way I wanted to break it to them.

The figure halted, came no closer. I could feel its gaze on me, though I could not see its eyes. *His* eyes. I felt suddenly sure it was a he, and the same ghost I had seen on the street earlier in the day.

"Who are you?" I yelled again, shuddering so hard the entire bed shook. "Brant Lamont?"

The figure laughed and I cringed reflexively. You'd think after all I've been through I'd be a poster child for ice-water nerves but no such luck. I was as scared as I got, and that was pretty damned scared.

He's coming...

I heard the words distinctly, whispered, snakelike and somehow threatening. At least they sounded threatening to me, but waking up naked to a shadowy ghost in your room in the dead of night will make you think Barney the dinosaur is threatening.

"What? Who? Who's coming? You mean 'She's coming', don't you? Ficatier?"

He's coming...unfinished business...

The shadowy figure wavered and the room grew colder.

Who knows what crimes cripple the mind of the guilty...

I was really starting to hate that phrase.

"It is you, Lamont, isn't it? What do you mean 'He's coming'? Who, if not Ficatier?"

Without a sound, the figure vanished and color splashed into the room again. I let out a relieved gasp but clutched the blankets tighter to my bosom.

Too afraid to move, I sat there for what seemed like an eternity, trying to draw deep breaths to get my composure back, but not having a hell of a lot of success. What the hell was that ghost up to? Why had I dreamt of Ficatier? Was she connected to the apparition? Had David really taken her head? Is that why she had been trying to work through Praetallious a few weeks an ago? Did it have to do with what Lansing had told me was coming and the escaped hell souls?

A noise pulled me from my thoughts and I peered at the end of the bed. Puddin' Head had opened one eye and was giving me "the look."

And it irritated me. Bad.

"I can't believe you freakin' slept through that!" I snapped at him, repressing the urge to kick him off the end of the bed.

FIFTEEN

Juicy Fruit, Bitter Fruit

11:45am...

Detective John Sturdevant was cramming an entire corner of a double-decker BLT into his mouth when he glanced up and saw me coming. Despite his mouth being full of sandwich, his expression dropped. Like I've said, I couldn't blame him. He was probably getting damn sick of me dumping my supernatural problems on his doorstep when Arly wasn't around. When he set the sandwich back in the plate, I noticed the life-weary look on his face; the look was even stronger than when I'd met him here at the diner yesterday morning. He'd been doing a lot of thinking about his life and former marriage and the advice I had given him. I recognized the signs, the haunted, lost look in the eyes, the dark half circles beneath them, the overall melancholy that seemed to flow from your very soul. I'd seen those signs all too many times staring back at me from my own mirror, whenever regrets over the way things had gone in my own life and the losses I had suffered got too much for me.

The lunch crowd had started to filter in and the place was noisier than I appreciated right now. As you might guess I hadn't really slept well after my little dream and the visitation by Mr. Black and Whispery. Not that it seemed to have bothered the cat much, because he had snored the rest of the night away and the few times I found myself dozing off abruptly ended with one of his resonant intakes. I should have kicked him out of the room. After all, he had half a dozen throw pillows scattered about my apartment, though of course he preferred to annex the end of my bed every night. He did it just to annoy me and prove his superiority, I'm fairly certain. I let him get away with it, so maybe he was right.

I guess it was better than sleeping by myself, though, when Arly was away. With that thought I glanced down at the engagement ring on my finger. I couldn't wait for the day when sleeping and waking up to ghosts and supernatural Boos alone was a thing of the past.

I tossed my backpack onto the booth seat and slid in behind it. Sturdevant wiped his mouth with a napkin and nodded.

"Chloe…"

I let out a chuckle. "You say that like I'm meeting you for an audit."

That almost got a smile out of him. "I think I'd prefer that."

"You wound me, Johnny." I laughed and accepted the coffee mug he pushed across the table. I grabbed the stainless steel pot and poured myself a cup.

"Not that I'm dying to know, but what is it this time?" He glanced at his sandwich as if he'd lost his appetite.

"Like I said on the phone, Lillian Marlene."

He nodded. "You also said there was something else you wanted to tell me about in person."

I glanced out through the window at the grayish day and suppressed a shiver. The clouds made everything look dull and gloomy and it reminded me of that black and white world I had been thrust into three times now. I reached up, grabbing my ponytail and pulling it to the front, then twisted the strands for a moment.

"Seems like there's always…something or things…"

"That fact hasn't escaped my attention," he said. "That's why they pay me the big detective bucks." He reached next to him on the seat and pulled up a manila folder, then slid it across the table.

"Lillian Marlene?" I asked.

He nodded. "What I could find, and there isn't a lot."

"Has to be more than I found on Lamont's fan page. They seem to have glossed over her."

He sighed, took a sip of his coffee. "I took a look. Most of those fans are cult fans, a little radical in their hero worship. I get the impression they blame the woman for his death and that's that."

"She was the last one to see him alive. Studying lines, supposedly."

He leaned back, shrugged. "That's the story. The file says a little different. She was thoroughly questioned at the time and under surveillance for a while afterward."

I glanced at the file. "What's it say?"

"She said they had a fight because Lamont wanted more from her than the actor mentor relationship."

I cocked an eyebrow. "They were photographed together and supposedly an item..."

"She claimed that was simply for publicity purposes, that Lamont was a closet homosexual and the studio wanted to make sure that didn't leak out."

"That true?"

He shrugged again. "Who knows? Things weren't so open in those days. He had quite a rep as a ladies' man, but so did Rock Hudson. Consensus was she was using him to further her career and according to her he was using her to further a façade. Had any proof of homosexuality gotten out at the time it would have killed any chance of a career revival."

"Something seems to have killed it and him anyway."

"We don't know he's dead."

"He was never heard from again. He just vanished and now I'm seeing his ghost. I'm thinking dead is a pretty good bet."

He let out a strained chuckle. "If I had to wager I'd go with dead, too. Seemed an odd time for him to simply walk off the face of the earth, since he was on the verge of reviving his career."

"What about suicide? I mean, his series got canceled, and he was stuck in his hometown theater."

"It's possible..."

I didn't like the hitch in his voice. "But you don't buy it?"

"I get the impression of an arrogant man who thought he was better than TV and certainly better than any small town theater. While it's true his career was in the dumper, rumor had it he was first in line for the lead villain in the upcoming Bond franchise. There was also talk of a *Sliver of Darkness* motion picture."

"Where'd you find this out?"

He ducked his chin at the folder. "It's in there. The detective at the time, a man name Pezzini, did his research. He didn't get much but what he got portrays a man not likely to off himself. He also noted he thought Marlene was lying to cover up something, though he wasn't sure what and couldn't prove it. There was no DNA testing in those days."

"This detective happen to be still be on the force? Could I talk to him?"

"You can, but he won't answer. He passed away in '72."

"Of what?"

"Lead poisoning. Took a bullet in the head during a robbery."

I nodded, frowned. "And Marlene, is she still alive?"

"I don't know yet. I'm running a check. It shouldn't be real hard to track down her eventual fate. File didn't have anything much past the initial investigation, and I couldn't find any film she was in beyond 1965. Reports had her suffering some sort of breakdown around that time, being impossible on sets, a real head case."

"Maybe Lamont's disappearance affected her more than she wanted to admit. Maybe she really did have a thing for him?"

"Maybe." He didn't sound entirely convinced, but whatever the case, damn little pointed me in a direction. I went silent for a moment, looking back out the window, sipping my coffee, wondering about Lamont and Marlene. Johnny interrupted my thoughts.

"You wanted to see me about more than Marlene, Chloe. You might as well come out with it."

I peered at him, a frown still creasing my lips. "I got a visit."

"From who? Or should I say what? Lamont?"

"Well, him, too."

"Who else?"

"A monkey."

SIXTEEN

Another Day at the Zoo

"**A**w, cripes!" Sturdevant pushed his sandwich away, his appetite now really shot. He fished in a suit pocket and pulled out a pack of Juicy Fruit.

"Tell me about it. I came home yesterday after meeting a friend to find Bob sitting on my coffee table."

He finished stuffing a piece of gum into his mouth, then returned the pack to his pocket. "You really need better locks."

"Like that'd stop a 600-year-old monkey or some old fogy ghost?"

"I see your point." He sighed. "So what'd Bob want this time? And why can't Lansing just be more direct?"

"I asked Bob that. He wasn't forthcoming. You know how closed-mouthed monkeys can be when they have a secret."

"That's real funny, Chlo. There's something damn peculiar about Lansing. I tried to contact her a couple times myself yesterday after-noon, figuring maybe she'd talk to me since she was avoiding you."

"And?"

"She's elusive, to say the least. Her assistant has an attitude, too. Gave me the runaround."

I nodded. "Apparently not big on modern inventions, such as the phone, either. But the Monkey Express left me another present."

He looked as if someone had hit him in the face with a hammer. "Another locket?"

"Not this time."

I reached for my backpack, unzipped the front pouch and rum-maged inside for the object Bob had set on my table. I pulled it out, a gold ring holding a black stone, then slid it across the table to him.

He peered at it as if it might have carried an electrical charge, then picked it up. "A ring?"

"Looks old. Has a bunch of symbols on it. Any idea what they mean?"

He peered intensely at it. "Looks like gibberish to me. Just slashes and angles and dots. Heavy enough piece. You seen it before?"

"Last thing that monkey gave me had a personal significance, but this…nothing I have ever seen. Certainly nothing that belonged to Pat; I'd remember something like that."

"There's…a face in the stone. It's vague. You can barely make it out…" His sigh came deeper this time, shuddering his entire frame. He passed the ring back to me. I stared at it myself a moment, then tapped it. I was betting it was at least a couple hundred years old, maybe more.

"You think that face belongs to who I think it does?" I was almost afraid to hear him confirm it.

Deep lines burrowed into his forehead and around his mouth. "Looks like the Devil."

I nodded. "That's what I thought. But all demons look kind of alike."

"Not to other demons, probably."

"I need Lansing to tell me what this is." I tapped the ring again.

"She doesn't seem fond of the direct route."

I chuckled without humor. "Sends her monkey to do her dirty work. Wish she'd include a note, at least."

"I wonder what her game is?" He sounded like he really didn't want the answer.

"I can't figure her out. She helps Arly, helps me, then hides in the shadows, vanishes from closed rooms, and seems to know way too much about things she should have no knowledge of."

"And is afraid of fire."

I nodded. "You know if I combine that fear of fire with a 600-hundred-year-old monkey and a knowledge of French antiques…"

He gave me a puzzled expression.

"Nevermind." I paused, glanced at the ring again, wondering what its significance was. Was it another protection symbol, like the locket? If so, why the devil face? I stuck the ring into my backpack and zipped it shut.

"There's more," I said, looking back to Sturdevant.

"Color me shocked."

"I had a dream."

"I had some too, none of them good. Most involved me getting chased by lawn gnomes."

I gave him a small laugh, still no humor in it but my nerves were frayed. I told him about the dream I'd had, how I had seen David walk away with Ficatier's head.

After I finished he leaned back, looking more distressed than ever. He had been there through the Sisters of the Snake thing and I don't think he had fully recovered. I guess, you never really get over something like that.

"It was just a dream, Chloe," he said at last, though his tone told me he didn't believe his own words. "She's dead."

"Dead doesn't matter much in this town, Johnny. Remember Chuckles the zombie?" Chuckles was a petty crook the Sisters of the Snake had reanimated and sent after me and Arly, for those of you not in the loop.

"Did you call David and ask him?"

"David's not so easy to call and talk to."

He nodded. "Have you tried?"

I frowned, shook my head. "No. It was a dream so I didn't really know how to even broach the subject to him and he's such an ass I'm not sure he'd give me a straight answer if he had one."

"He did help Arlo defeat Ficatier. Why would he take her head?"

I shrugged, took a sip of coffee. "I don't know. Maybe he wouldn't. And maybe it was just a dream. But it didn't feel like a dream."

"I hear you. But Ficatier *is* dead. She's not coming back."

"I saw her in Praetallious' eyes, Johnny. She's trying to come back. I'm damn near certain of it."

"Have you talked to Arlo about this?"

I shook my head, my stomach tightening. "No. I got hold of him early this morning but left out anything about dreams and black and white ghosts. If I told him he'd just come running back wanting to save me. This is the first vacation he's had in ages. I don't want to ruin it."

"Might ruin it a whole lot worse if you got yourself killed."

"Would be worse if I got *him* killed. I don't want to see him in the hospital that way again. It was too hard."

"He'd disagree."

"I know he would."

Sturdevant's eyes turned sad and his face got even more serious, if that were possible. "Yesterday you gave me advice about what to do about my family, so let me return the favor. It's painfully obvious I'm no relationship expert, Chloe, but I can tell you this: you and Arlo can't go around keeping things from each other, or trying to protect one another by keeping secrets. It won't work. Take it from someone who lost what was most dear to him. Sooner or later it will catch up to you and what you have…that'll go away, or at least it will become too hard to live with."

He was right and I knew it. "Did you call her?"

He gazed down at the table, a guilty expression coming onto his face. "No, not yet. I'm still thinking about it. She may not want to hear from me. She may not want my excuses."

"Then don't give her any. Give her the truth. And don't put it off for too long."

He looked up, eyebrows raised. "You think I don't see that you're trying to change the subject?"

I laughed, more genuine this time. "I figured I was being clever."

"I'm a detective, remember? The badge says so."

I smiled, paused. "I saw Lamont last night, too."

"Before your dream?"

"After. I woke up to see him, or at least I think it was him, standing in my room and everything was black and white again."

"You sure you weren't just lucid dreaming? Maybe it was left over from your nightmare."

After another sip of coffee, I shook my head. "I'm sure. I don't even know if his appearance had anything to do with Ficatier or if she is something I'm going to have to deal with in the future. He said something to me, too, and it had nothing to do with her."

"What'd he say?"

"He said 'He's coming…'"

"He? You mean, she? Ficatier?"

"That's what I thought he meant at first, but he said 'he', not she."

"Don't you have enough demons and ghosts in your life? You need something else coming? What, another one of those things that supposedly escaped when Arlo lopped off Ficatier's head? Is Lamont one of those?"

A sudden wave of exhaustion washed over me and I leaned back, everything catching up to me. Dreams and demons, ghosts and missing sisters. How much was too much? "I don't know if I'm strong enough to keep this up, Johnny."

He let out a laugh that was almost natural. "The hell you aren't. You're stronger than me and Arlo put together, Chlo. Otherwise you would have got your ass out of this pissy town ages ago."

I would have liked to believe him but right now I felt anything but strong. I felt lost and vulnerable and like I was chasing another will-'o-the-wisp.

"I hope you're right." My voice didn't hold much confidence.

"I *am* right. But you should tell Arlo what's going on just the same."

"I'll think about it." Translation: not bloody likely. At least not at this point. I wasn't going to risk him, even if what Johnny had said was true. I couldn't lose him. I had lost too damn much in my life already.

I stood, grabbed the folder Sturdevant had brought me and my backpack. I slung the backpack over a shoulder.

He frowned up at me. "Don't get yourself killed, Chlo. I've been to enough funerals over the past few months."

"It isn't on my 'To Do' list for the day." I winked. "But it's nice to feel the love."

"Love, shmuv, I just don't want to have to explain to Arlo why I didn't tell him you were chasing demons and ghosts on your own."

"Detective-stripper confidentially…"

"There's no such thing."

"There should be."

"I'll take it up with the captain."

I gave him a serious look. "Call your wife, Johnny…*today.*"

Another big frown from him told me he might not take my advice. "What's your next step?" he asked, avoiding the subject.

I smiled. "I'm off to see the pixie, and her little monkey, too…"

SEVENTEEN

Pixie Non Grata

The interior of the New Salem Museum of Natural History always made me want to retch and today was no exception. My shoes clacked on the tiled flooring, which had recently been redone in tie-dye and I seriously considered yakking into my backpack, but refrained because that would only make me need to buy a new backpack. The pink and green neon light strings on the walls cast a nauseating glare throughout the reception area and accentuated the Oh-Christ-here-she-comes-again expression on the punky receptionist's face. The young woman's hair color was far too close to the salmon-colored walls and too damn many piercings ran along either ear.

I went straight for her, unable to deny the feeling of satisfaction her dissatisfaction gave me.

"I want to see Lansing—now," I said, making my voice no-nonsense. I unzipped my backpack flap and pulled out the ring, clanked it on the counter top. "About this."

"It's a ring," the spike-haired young woman said and I didn't care much for her tone. It said I was an imbecile.

"And I thought Lansing only hired you for your looks."

Her expression changed a bit, went into Rosie O'Donnell mode, if you get my drift. She tucked strands of hair behind a multi-pierced ear, neon light reflecting from her Minnie Mouse watch.

"Don't even think it," I said, instantly wiping the expression off her thin little lips.

She shrugged. "Too bad."

No, it's not too bad at all, I thought. If I were even inclined to swing that way I would pick a chick with smaller testicles.

"Buzz her," I said, trying not to let my annoyed nerves get the better of me.

"She's not in."

"She's never frickin' in." My voice went up a notch. "Every time I call she's conveniently in a meeting or out on a buy."

She gave me a prissy little smile. I *reeeaaallly* wanted to slap her. "She's a whirlwind of activity."

Ok, now that was just plain snotty. And it pissed me off. Big time. I grabbed the ring, jammed it into my backpack and zipped the compartment shut.

"I'm done with you," I said, flinging my pack over a shoulder.

"Hey, you can't just—" she started as I stepped around the counter and beelined for the long hallway leading to Lansing's office.

"You could try to stop me," I said over my shoulder, "But you'll need an ass plumber to pull your Minnie Mouse watch out of the place I cram it."

She didn't try to stop me but a word flew out of her mouth referring to a particular part of the female anatomy I rarely heard come out of a woman, even with some of the low-end strippers I'd worked with. She'd said it under her breath but things carried in this place. Normally for that I would have made good on my threat but I had enough on my mind to let her off the hook. *This* time. I swore if I had to deal with her again, though, I was gong to go all stripper on her skinny little boy ass.

My steps clattered in the long hallway and a sudden chill shivered through me. Not really fear, just…I don't know what it was, honestly. Something about this place and something about Genie Lansing just gave me the jitters. Someday I was going to figure out that woman and when I did I had the feeling I wasn't going to like it. I had started to get some ideas, but I'd confront her with them another time. Today, I'd settle for just getting her to tell me what this ring was for and why she kept having her little sidekick do her dirty work. And maybe I'd try asking her about Pat again while I was at it. She knew more than she was telling and I think that was the major reason she was avoiding me.

I noticed her office door was open a crack and I hoped that was a good sign the receptionist had been lying to me about Lansing being out.

I took a deep breath, setting my attitude dial to bitchy because if she were in the office I knew I was going to need all my composure. She had this way of getting under my skin, and part of that had to do with her crushin' on my man.

I pushed the door open with the flat of my hand like I was storming into the boss's office to demand a raise.

Genie Lansing wasn't in the room.

But guess who was?

EIGHTEEN

Monkey See, Monkey Go

"**Y**ou been promoted?" I asked Bob, who sat atop Lansing's desk doing that crinkly monkey thing with his forehead. He didn't seem particularly surprised to see me, which creeped me out a little.

"Where's your mom, or whatever she is to you?" I asked, stopping just inside the door.

Bob apparently wasn't in a chatty mood, because he just stared at me.

I gazed about the room, not really thinking Lansing would be hiding in a corner but more out of a what-the-hell-do-I-do-now? feeling. I mean, storming into a place and demanding to see the owner worked a hell of a lot better when said owner was in the damn building. If you know what I mean.

I stepped deeper into the room, frowning, stopping in front of the desk.

"Where the hell is she, Bob?" I asked. "Why'd she send you to my apartment with a ring? Your owner's got some damn strange habits, you know that?"

Bob kept doing the forehead thing.

"And you...you're how old?"

Bob jumped off the desk, scooted across the office floor and out of the room. I had the weird feeling I'd insulted him.

"Why the hell are you trying to have a conversation with a monkey, anyway?" I asked myself.

As I stood there, an eerie sensation of being watched came over me. I glanced about the room again but it was as empty as it had been a moment ago. Unless Lansing was invisible. The thought that that might not be out of the realm of possibility didn't do my nerves any good. She *did* have a distressing way of just appearing in places.

I tried to shake off the feeling, losing much of lather I had worked up.

Great. She really *wasn't* here. Now what was I going to do? Why couldn't she just tell me what the damn ring was for instead of making me run around in circles?

Good or bad? I asked myself again. Was Lansing on the plus or minus side?

I glanced at her desk, then back over my shoulder at the door, a thought occurring to me. I padded to the door, like being quiet was really going to help after I'd clomped my way down the hall. I figured I wouldn't have very long before Ms. Punk-a-Doodle got her butt down here to see what I was up to. I didn't think I had scared her that bad. She had sounded more pissed off than scared, judging by her choice of language.

I eased the door shut and went back to the desk. I set my backpack atop it and went around to its front. The thing had a number of drawers and oddly enough none of them had locks.

"Who are you, Genie Lansing?" I whispered and pulled open the top drawer.

To say I was disappointed was an understatement. I don't know what I expected to find but an empty drawer wasn't it. Not even a pencil or pen or one of her plastic bracelets was inside.

I closed it and tugged open another. Empty again. I went through every drawer and each was bare.

Who the hell's desk was full of empty drawers?

"Ok," I whispered, "you just got even more mysterious."

Crap on a cracker. It was like nobody even used the desk.

I figured my time was about up and I went to grab my backpack. There was nothing else I could do here and I wasn't going to wait around all day for Pixie Sticks to show up. I had no idea if she'd even be in today.

As I reached for my backpack I noticed a large opened book and few scattered papers atop the desk blotter. In fact, now that I thought about it, Bob had been sitting on the book, hadn't he?

I moved my backpack and glanced at the opened page. It showed a photo of a London Newspaper, the *Evening Star,* dated 1888. I read the first few lines, then flipped the page. The next page contained a particularly gruesome morgue picture of a murdered prostitute named Mary Kelly. I closed the book, a little sickened at the site of the mutilated victim. Composing myself, I examined some of the other papers on the desk. Each pertained to some aspect of a murder occurring in Whitechapel, England in the late 1880s.

"Jack the Ripper?" I muttered, a chill going through me for no reason I could pinpoint. Why would Genie Lansing be interested in Jack the Ripper? A killer who had lived and mostly likely died over a century ago. Was she planning some grisly exhibit, since he was a part of history? That seemed like something you'd more likely find in a wax museum, not one on natural history, though she did have some odd choices of exhibits in the place.

From beyond the closed door I heard footsteps clomping down the hall. Ms. Punk-a-Doodle walked with all the grace of a drunken horse.

I scooted around to the front of the desk just as the door whisked open.

"What are you doing?" the receptionist asked, her tone not even close to pleasant.

"Lansing's not here," I said stupidly, trying to keep any hint of guilt over having searched the desk out of my own voice.

"I told you that." She folded her arms and tried to look tough. She kind of reminded me of a pug.

I smiled the patronizing little smile I liked to give stuck-up tweaks with implants. "So you did. And you were right, too."

"You should leave." She looked at me like I was rat poison and she was queen rat.

"What a coincidence, I was just on my way out."

As I stepped forward the young woman's gaze never left me. I think she was ogling my boobs. I wasted no time brushing past her and starting down the hall. I could feel her gaze drilling into my backside, probably a lot lower on my anatomy than I felt comfortable with, but didn't turn around.

NINETEEN

Underneath the Dancelight

The usual crowd packed the Red Lagoon by the time the first stripper took the stage. I had come in an hour late, having gotten hung up putting the finishing touches on my costume, but I wasn't scheduled to go on until eight anyway. Pete had gone all out for Disco Night. I didn't quite understand his fascination with the period, but he had this thing about decorating for holidays, so I figured it had something to do with the whole theme fixation or maybe he was just neurotic. There's a fine line.

I spotted a drunk hanging onto the edge the stage that jutted out into the center of the room, whooping at the small-breasted, black-haired girl—her name was Callie and she was a recent addition, one I guessed wouldn't be here long since she was just earning some quick money for college—dancing to a Donna Summer song that thumped from the twin overhead speakers. Pete, Bee Gees bless him, had installed a glittering disco ball overhead and even a few laser lights for my routine. I gave the drunk roughly another fifteen minutes before Pete tossed him out on his ass for trying to grope one of the girls.

This was one of those nights when I wondered why I still bothered to do what I do. I enjoy dancing, don't get me wrong, and I enjoy the feeling of control, or, like I said, I used to enjoy it. Not so much now that I was going to marry Arly. I had quit a few weeks ago, only going back to it when I needed a job that allowed me the freedom to track down Praetallious. I'd stayed because in the back of my mind my stripper sense told me it wouldn't be long before some other hellish escapee appeared on my doorstep and I guess I had been proved right. So I still needed something that permitted me to come and go when I pleased, and I *did* have bills to pay. It would be different when Arly and I got married and I lived with him. I could find something else. But I just wasn't feeling the same about my profession now and the thought of guys ogling me was getting more and more...I don't know, maybe *old* is the word I'm looking for.

Holding out my hand, fingers splayed, I glanced down at my engagement ring, mesmerized for a moment by how the lights from the danceball reflected off of it. I'm like a lot of women, despite what you may think. I wanted to be married, have that fairytale love. I couldn't wait to start my new life with Arly. But somehow I knew the fairytale might be a whole lot closer to Brothers Grimm than Cinderella. We weren't exactly a normal couple. I mean, normal couples didn't go around getting kidnapped by evil witches and chased by zombies, right?

Or visited by old-time actor ghosts.

I leaned against the bar, letting out a sigh. The music changed to *Dancing Queen* by ABBA as Callie left the stage and Amanda came on. I watched her for a moment, noting her stride was still that awkward colt gait I remembered. She hadn't had time to design any kind of special costume, so she was wearing a regular pull-away skirt and tied-beneath-the-boobs blouse. Her cleavage swung like it had a life of its own and the drunk at the bar got a lot louder. Like I said, what she didn't have in natural dancing talent she made up for in porch and the men were just as pleased as punch.

I saw Pete throw the drunk a look. He was pretty close to hauling the guy out and was keeping a wary eye on a couple others starting to act up. I knew he'd exchanged the Louisville for a shotgun, which he kept below the counter like an Old West barkeep, just in case another pervert turned out to be a girlfriend killer like the guy I told you about. Usually he had Arly toss out that type when Arly was here, which he was only on nights I danced now and he was lucky I let him get away with that. If anybody's ever told you strippers don't get jealous of their men looking at other women naked don't believe them. It's a double standard, considering what I'm showing off, but it annoyed the hell out of me and as Amanda whipped off her top I was suddenly really glad he was out of town. I mean, *realllyyy* glad. Bad enough I had to contend with little Ms. Pixie Sticks crushin' on my man, I didn't need competition in the ta-ta department.

"She's good, Chlo," Pete said, grabbing a glass and wiping it out.

"Huh?" I said, coming from my thoughts.

He ducked his chin at Amanda. "Marlene, she's good, I said. Thanks for sending her my way."

I gave him a "Yeah, right" smirk. "Sure, Pete. You get past her boobs?"

He flashed me a guilty grin. "Do I have to?"

I laughed, shook my head. "Why should you?"

Wait a minute. What had he called her? Had I just heard wrong because the name was in the back of my mind?

"You mean Amanda Connors is good?" I said it a little tentatively, in case I had heard wrong and didn't want him thinking I was losing my mind.

"Connors?" He gave me a puzzled raise of the eyebrow. "You mean Amanda Marlene..."

He *had* said Marlene. I glanced at the stage. She was down to a G-string and the drunk made his move. He reached for her, somehow missing, though I couldn't quite figure out how, because she was leaning right over him and he was stuffing a dollar into her string. She was suddenly upright and a perplexed look washed across the drunk's face.

I looked back to Pete. "That's Amanda Connors."

He shrugged. "Told me her name was Amanda Marlene. I don't care what it is with that—"

I cut him off. "I get it, Pete."

"Now, if you'll excuse me..." Pete went around the bar and headed towards the drunk. The Lagoon was about to be minus one lubed patron because Pete had seen the grab he made at Amanda's porch. But right now that was the farthest thing from my mind because my stripper sense was tingling again with the name Marlene. Amanda Marlene. Lillian Marlene. What the hell?

TWENTY

A Strip in Time

The sound of horns and laser sears blared and sizzled from the overhead speakers as the lights lowered in the Lagoon. The ball whirled, splashing the room with variegated diamonds as beams of light flashed from its mirrored surface. Meco's disco *Theme from Star Wars* throbbed into full gear as I strode out onto the stage, my curves enveloped in a flowing white robe slit on both sides to show generous flashes of my bare legs as I strutted my stuff. The robe covered me from neck to toe, as close to the one Princess Leia had worn in the movie as I could get without being hauled away by the infringement police. I'd pinned my hair into cinnamon rolls to either side of my head and the only thing I was missing was a cardboard cutout of R2D2 to make the illusion completely cheesy enough to satisfy Pete.

I'd like to say the crowd went wild but I think they had put away too many beers to appreciate the craftsmanship of my routine. They wanted flesh and a heaping helping of it, which I fortunately had. I sometimes wondered why I bothered to put so much effort into costumes and routines that just resulted in me getting 95 percent naked, but I suppose I'm a frustrated artist at heart. I still longed for the craft of burlesque, the old bump and grind, instead of the titillation and seedier aspects associated with strippers, excuse me, exotic dancers, nowadays.

I sashayed down the center of the stage, my hands going to my head and plucking out the pins that held up my hair. My blonde locks cascaded down over my shoulders. I could barely see the faces gawking at me with the lights flashing all about the stage. I heard whooping above the music. Another drunk on his way to a sidewalk pass.

I pursed my lips, winked and whirled, striding back up the stage, turning again, coming back.

The male psyche is a strange and perverted thing, I'll give it that. It probably takes about the same effort to get their attention with a pair of hooters as it does to get Bob's focus with something shiny. Women aren't quite as visually oriented as men, but I suppose I should be thankful for that because it allowed me to make a hell of a lot more money than I would have working as a secretary. And most corporations wouldn't let me play dress up, so that was a plus.

But like I said, I had started to feel different about it and it was getting harder to do the big reveal. Maybe I was just going through a mid-life crisis a little early or the fact that I was now engaged really had changed me more than I thought. The sense of power and control over my world, over men, had shifted in many respects. With Arly, I felt like I had a place to belong, to be safe—well, as safe as it was possible to be when the supernatural was constantly nipping at your naughty bits—stability, I guess I could call it. I had never felt that way after losing my parents and Pat and being bounced around in the foster home system, then on my own in the circuit for so many years. I just didn't need the false sense of self-esteem stripping gave me as much as I used to.

Although I did have stripping to thank for attracting Arly to me. I knew that. He knew that, too, but the moment he'd laid eyes on me I had seen more, because unlike most of the men in this place, he'd been looking into my eyes, not at my chest or ass. That made him different, in fact, unique among the men I'd met in my profession, or otherwise. It made him special.

Coming from my thoughts—my routine had continued by remote control, because I have done this for so many years it was automatic now—I grabbed both sides of the flowing robe and yanked. It had Velcro sidings and the garment parted in two pieces. I windmilled both sections in opposite directions, then let them flutter to the stage floor. Beneath the robe I wore a sequined silver and blue halter and a tinsel skirt of multi-colored sequins above my G-string. The flashing lights glinted off my top and skirt like I was radioactive and sparkled like variegated fireflies across the stage. The whoops increased, because, let's face it, even at 36 everything was still perfectly where it should be and I was built like a frickin' brick house.

I swirled my hips in a figure eight, drew my splayed fingers up my glitter-sprayed belly, then over my sequined halter top. I lifted my blonde hair and let it fall back seductively, then grabbed the pole in the center of the stage and whirled around it. After wrapping my legs about the pole, I arched my back, released my hands and leaned all the way back until my palms touched the floor. One of the drunks looked about ready to make a grab at a ta-ta so I flashed him a look hot enough to scorch off his eyebrows and he thought better of it.

I came back up, grabbed the pole and swung myself around again, then hit the stage on my high heels. My fingers went to the clasp in the center of my top. I took a deep breath to steady a sudden burst of butterflies—yes, even after all these years there are nights I get a few butterflies showing the goods and tonight, for some reason, was one of them.

My top came off, but it suddenly didn't matter. Because the nerves in my belly no longer came from releasing the girls. They came from something else, something that froze me with my halter in my hand and my heart in my throat. The Lagoon flashed to black and white and the music changed.

"Oh, Calcutta…" I whispered.

TWENTY-ONE

Who Knows What Crimes?

Calcutta now chimed from the twin speakers instead of Meco and I suddenly felt entirely silly standing there holding my spangled top in one hand, both girls gleaming in all their black and white glory. The light overhead still turned, but flashed stark diamond stars across the audience.

The audience. The audience now dressed in clothing over forty years out of date. I even spotted a few women in the audience, their dresses and bouffant hairdos indicating I'd stepped back into the '60s again. I shot a glance at the bar but Pete was no longer there. In his place stood some other bartender, wearing a tux. The Lagoon looked far more like a dinner club than a topless joint.

I recall Pete having told me that back in the '60s the place used to be just that, a dinner club catering to patrons who wandered in before or after New Salem Theater performances.

I suddenly dropped the spangled halter and folded my arms across my breasts, because, crap, now I felt *really* naked. Again. Here I was topless in a dinner theater and it felt like being caught wearing your pajamas to school. I swear I would have actually been embarrassed if it hadn't been for the fact I was again startled out of my G-string.

The people didn't seem to be looking at me; that was the only consolation. They went on about their business, chatting, clinking glasses, laughing, women leaning in and kissing their husbands or boyfriends on the cheek. It was almost as if I didn't exist to them, or was somehow invisible.

I shivered, then, for above the music echoed a laugh, sibilant and eerie. I am not sure how I even heard it over the chiming harpsichords and high voices, but I did, ghostly and clear.

The laugh strengthened and the music lowered. My gaze went to a spot near the door; a figure in a black cape and slouch hat stood there, face shadowy and form menacing. The same figure who'd appeared in my bedroom last night.

His hand drifted up, all dramatic-like, and I knew it had to be Lamont. It had that actor's flare, that *old time* actor's flare. And as silly as it might have looked, it still carried a weird power that sent waves of coldness through my belly. Along with the coldness came a wave of sadness, depression that I was certain emanated from the apparition.

He's coming...

The voice shuddered out, sending more chills through me. My legs went a little soupy and I clutched my arms about my bosom even tighter. If I had had implants they would have popped.

"What to you want?" I forced myself to say, hoping my voice wouldn't shake, but it did. A lot. "Who? Who's coming?"

Unfinished business...

I tried to get control over my nerves. I felt an inch away from turning and bolting but I was too compulsively curious to do that.

"What do you want, Lamont? Why have you come back? Who's unfinished business? Yours? Marlene's?"

That fact that Pete had told me Amanda had used the last name Marlene didn't escape me just then. I wondered whether this visitation was somehow connected with her and you can bet I was going to call her on it at the proper moment and get her to do some explaining.

But the thought zipped out of my mind for the time being because with the mention of Marlene's name the figure wavered. Yes, I mean wavered, like a bad TV image. He just sort of flowed side to side in waves from top to bottom for a moment, becoming insubstantial.

Then he was back and his slouch-hatted head lifted. I still couldn't clearly see his face because it was blurred, shadowy, though somewhat sharper than when I had glimpsed it on the street. I could tell he had a hooked nose and I was now more certain than ever it was Lamont.

Marlene...

It wasn't exactly hate that came with the whispered name, more like utter bitterness, or perhaps throbbing regret. I wasn't certain, but it was something exquisitely unpleasant.

He's here...

That stopped my thoughts dead. Damn, dead wasn't the best choice of words, was it? In fact it was a damn poor choice but I got no time to think about it because suddenly everything was in color again and Meco throbbed from the speakers.

I was still standing in the middle of the stage with my arms wrapped across my boobs but the regular crowd was back and staring at me like I was a clown on a bus. My eyes widened as I took in all the bemused faces—and a few of irritated ones because I was covering the goods. Behind the bar, Pete had stopped polishing a glass and was looking over, concern on his face. My mouth came open, closed again, and I gritted my teeth. I am not sure how I even made it through the rest of my routine.

TWENTY-TWO

After the Disco Ball

I don't think I have ever been so happy for a routine to be over with. I don't think I have ever shaken that much through a dance bit, either, at least not since the first few times I hit the stage when I was in my teens. But I was glad to get through it, and glad I had gotten back into my jeans and a blue T-shirt. I'd stuffed my *Star Wars* getup into a trunk and waited in my dressing room the rest of the night until Pete was getting ready to close. My dressing room was small with a vanity, a couple old steamer trunks, a saucer chair and changing partition, plus a 12-inch TV that sometimes worked and sometimes didn't.

I had switched on every light in the room, in fact, having little wish to have anything that even remotely resembled a shadow in here with me. I couldn't believe Lamont had shown up at the Lagoon. It was bad enough the supernatural showed up at my house but couldn't it give me a frickin' break at work? I had looked foolish on stage tonight and the only redeeming factor was that most of the men had been too drunk to give a damn. But I did. Because I knew, *knew*, no one else in that room had seen what I had seen. No one had glimpsed the ghost of Brant Lamont and no one had noticed the world had changed to black and white. If I wasn't so sure it was a supernatural event I really would have thought I was going nuts.

A knock sounded on the dressing room door and I turned from the track-lit mirror to see the door open a crack.

Pete's voice asked, "Are you decent?"

"I've been working here for how long and you just get around to asking?" I tried to make my voice light, but a tremor seeped in.

Pete stuck his big head into the room. "You sure you're all right, Chlo?" His face held concern. He was every stripper's dad and he really did care.

"I'm fine," I lied, and I know he could tell.

"You're not fine. You want me to call Arlo?"

"No!" I said, too fast. I most certainly did not want him to call Arly. That's just what I needed, him rushing back to save me and getting himself smack in the middle of whatever this was. "I'm fine, Pete, really. Just caught a touch of some bug or something."

"In the middle of your routine?" he asked, clearly dubious. "You just stopped dead on the stage for a couple minutes, Chloe. Just stood there."

Dead. There was that damn word again. He didn't know how close he had come to the truth. "I felt like I was going to hurl. Didn't think you'd want me yakking on the customers."

He uttered a sharp laugh. "Like they'd notice. Half of them were ready to hurl themselves. I know, 'cause a couple did after I hauled their butts out to the sidewalk for trying to touch one of the girls."

I hesitated, wondering whether I should ask Pete what had happened during those few minutes, then decided what the hell. "Pete, did anything...anything odd happen while I was sanding there?"

His brow furrowed. "Odd? Odd, how?"

"Odd as in..." Oh, great, how was I going to ask him about everything turning colorless. "Was everything in color?"

"Huh?" Confusion danced over his full face. "What do you mean, was everything in color?"

I shook my head. "Nevermind, it was a dumb question. Still not feeling well, I guess."

Another "yeah, right" look. "This isn't another one of those, you know, *things* Arlo and you get into, is it?"

"It might be, Pete." I wasn't about to lie to him on that. He'd know better anyway.

He drew his face back from the door, sighed. "You watch yourself, Chloe. Too many weird things going on lately. I don't want what happened to Bettina back during that witch thing happening to you. You're like a daughter to me."

I laughed. "How many dads hire their daughters to take their clothes off, Pete?"

"That's a little creepy, Chloe. You know what I mean."

I nodded, smiling a genuine smile. "Yeah, I do know and I appreciate the hell out of it. You're like my family."

He laughed. "Speaking of which, when the hell you going to get hitched and invite me to the wedding, anyway?"

I stood, grabbing my backpack from another chair. "You and Sturd can fight Arly for the best man position."

"I can throw a better bachelor party."

"Uh-huh, well, don't. Arly gets into enough trouble all on his own."

"You almost sound jealous, Chlo. A stripper jealous, who'd a thunk it?"

"Me, jealous? Don't even go there." I turned, switched off the mirror lights. "Oh, Pete," I said over my shoulder.

"Yeah," he said, as I turned toward him.

"Amanda leave yet?"

He shook his head. "Far as I know she's still in her dressing room."

I thanked him and he wandered off. I stood in the room a moment, almost afraid to go out into the dark night. I knew Pete must have already closed up and would be within yelling distance, but it hadn't left my mind there was still a ripper on the loose.

A noise from the hall caught my attention and I hurried to the door. I saw Amanda just coming out of her room, a macramé purse slung over her shoulder. Macramé? And I thought my jean backpack was kitschy.

"Hey," she said, spotting me looking at her.

I flicked off the light switch, then pulled the door shut. "Was thinking of going over to the diner for coffee. You want to come with me?"

She shook her head, a thin smile creasing her lips. "I should be getting back to my aunt's cottage. I'm still going through trunks and things."

The problem here was no matter how nicely I had put it I really didn't want to give her a choice. I needed some answers about her last name. I hesitated, because the sadness haunted her eyes again, along with something else, something I couldn't really put a finger on.

"I really need to talk to you, Amanda. Tonight." I made my voice firm and she appeared slightly taken aback.

"Can it wait?"

"It shouldn't." I was ready to use the I-got-you-this stinking-job card, but didn't have to.

She nodded. "Ok, I guess I could for a little while."

I smiled, came down the dingy hall and we headed for the back door. As I stepped out into the night the strangest feeling of dread swelled from deep in my belly. Shadows everywhere, stretching from cars and from building corners in the back parking lot, which was lit by a single pole lamp. It occurred to me somebody could be hiding in any of a hundred places and I almost expected the world to switch to black and white again. But it didn't. It was just my nerves making my stripper sense go off, I told myself. Amanda didn't seem to notice. She had a sort of odd, blank look on her face.

He's coming...

Lamont's words jumped into my mind and I hesitated in my step.

"Something wrong?" Amanda said, not even looking at me.

"No, I just..." I just what? I didn't have an explanation, did I?

A sound. Like a scuffing of a foot, and I shuddered again. Had I even heard it or was my mind just playing tricks on me?

"You hear anything?" I asked, avoiding answering her question.

"No," she said, voice low, almost distant, like she was somewhere else.

"Which one's your car?" I asked, trying to shake off the feeling.

"My car?" she said, a note of surprise jumping into her voice. She was acting a little weird and I wondered why. Maybe it was just first night in a new place jitters or maybe she was on something. A lot of strippers I knew took something to get them through their routines but Amanda hadn't really looked the type.

"Your car. What you drove here in." I hoped I wasn't making her sound like a dunce.

"I...I walked, actually." I couldn't tell if she were lying. A number of cars still occupied the back lot, some of them belonging to an apartment building across from it, its backside lightless. A thin cobbled side street ran to the left, flanked by the brick wall of a closed Japanese import shop.

"You walked all the way from the cottage? With a ripper on the loose?"

She nodded, and finally a smile came to her face. "I like walking. It helps me not think of my...aunt. How likely is it any ripper will bother me anyway?"

I felt like saying, well, that was just plain stupid, because he had more than bothered a number of young women on the waterfront lately, so why take chances? I still looked in the back seat of my car every night, even though I locked it, because in every damn horror movie where a young girl gets into an unlocked car somebody jumps out of the back seat and slashes her throat.

But I didn't have to say anything because just as we made it half-way across the parking lot the whole how-likely-was-a-ripper-to-bother-you argument became moot.

TWENTY-THREE

Yours Truly, Carlis the Ripper

A figure stepped from behind a car. It just seemed to emerge from the shadows, almost like a...

Ghost?

Whatever. He was there and coming at us and I caught a glint of light from a knife in his right hand.

I reacted on instinct and was about to shove Amanda backward, but she somehow floated back out of his way, almost as if she had expected him to be there.

That was a stupid thought, I told myself, but didn't get any time to dwell on it because the guy was suddenly in front of me.

I pivoted out of his way, but he turned faster than I would have thought possible. I caught the whiff of something horrible, a stench of the dead, decay, like the one that had clung to that zombie Arly and I had run into with the Sisters of the Snake.

I scrambled backward, whipping my backpack from my shoulder, intending to swing it as a weapon. It was heavy enough, but wouldn't do much good other than maybe stop a knife thrust if I timed it right and I doubted I was that coordinated. I still had weeks of karate classes ahead of me before reaching that level. Assuming I lived through tonight, which at the moment didn't look like a hell of a good prospect.

The figure was a man, definitely, though cloaked in shadow. He wore some sort of tank top, torn, dirty white, and jeans. This was no Victorian stalker in a deerstalker cap. The knife in his hand appeared to be a switchblade, but I wasn't certain.

He lunged and I screeched. I know, not real brave, but the dude had a frickin' knife and had brutally sliced up a number of women already.

I was terrified of knives. I always had been. More so than guns, even. And more so since I'd nearly been sacrificed to a demon last fall.

I managed to stumble backward and keep my backpack in front of me, but my ass hit a car door and there was no place else to go.

I caught a glimpse of Amanda and she was just standing there, looking stupid. I told myself it was just terror freezing her, but wished to hell she would run and get Pete.

To compensate for that I let out a scream at the top of my lungs. I think it could be heard in Massachusetts.

It didn't bother the ripper dude one bit, though. He uttered a soft laugh and for an instant his face came into the light and everything inside me froze. I suddenly could not have protected myself had I wanted to because I was too much in shock. His face, though it was half covered with open rotting sores and patches of bone showed through, was one I recognized and to say I was the most terrified I had ever been might not have been an exaggeration, and I have been through some crap, let me tell you.

"Remember me?" he asked, his voice harsh, grating…dead.

Dead. I really frickin' hated that word.

His knife came up and I stood there, my backside pressed against a car door, like deer in the headlights. Every part of me shook and I couldn't even lift my backpack as the knife plunged towards me.

TWENTY-FOUR

He'll Take a Double

I was deadmeat and I knew it. I was too terrified to move, despite the fact a knife was plunging towards me. I think instead of my life flashing before my eyes I actually saw crinkly-headed monkeys and maybe even Mr. Buggles the clown laughing a final goodbye, his pants still wrapped around his bony knees.

Things happened in a lightning-swift storm of movement, and through some heightened awareness born of terror I took in every detail, including the realization that the man driving a knife towards my chest could not possibly be standing in front of me, yet he most certainly was. That really shouldn't have shocked me as much as it did. Not in this town.

He's here…

Lamont's words rang through my mind and now I knew what he'd meant. He had been warning me, not threatening me, but in another moment that would not matter, because I had figured it out too late.

Then a clap of thunder roared through the parking lot. The crashing boom slammed into my eardrums and shook me from my terror-induced spell. I jerked sideways, out of the way of the descending blade, but the move proved to be unnecessary because the ripper staggered to his left a few steps and the knife shrieked across the hood of the car, ruining somebody's paint job.

Half the killer's side turned into a gruesome patch of mangled flesh, flesh that was too deeply gray to be living tissue, and part of this tank top shredded.

I glanced towards the back door to see Pete, bleached hands clenched about a shotgun, grimace on his face, taking aim at the ripper for a second time.

The killer straightened, turned back towards me.

Pete triggered a second blast that hit the ripper flush in the chest. I probably don't have to describe what damage a shotgun blast will do to a body at such a close range. It makes a frickin' mess. I'd never really seen it, except in a horror movie, but I knew it wouldn't be pretty just the same. The blast tore the rest of the guy's tank top to ribbons, along with a good portion of his chest. No blood came from the wounds, just icky gray stuff. The impact kicked him back a number of paces and he flashed me an odd smile, then whirled and ran. An instant later darkness swallowed him.

I shuddered harder than I ever had in my life. I seriously thought I was going to just shake myself apart and might have if it hadn't been for Pete's sudden and loud, "What the goddamn hell?"

He stared after the fleeing killer, the shotgun smoking from both barrels and shock doing a crappy dance on his face. He'd fired both those barrels into the killer, yet the man had run off like he'd merely been sprayed with a garden hose.

I could have told him there was a damn good reason for that, but I didn't think he was ready to hear it.

"I fired both barrels at him..." Pete's words came low, filled with incredulity, and I knew his mind was groping for a reasonable explanation, but I had none to offer. "He couldn't have just run away."

And yet...my gaze shifted to Amanda, who still just stood there, peering after the fleeing killer. Little emotion period registered on her face and I attributed that to shock, the shock of what had happened and the shock of seeing her it-won't-happen-to-me theory bolting out into the night.

"Amanda, you all right?" I asked and she nodded slowly, then more emotion came into her face.

"I was wrong..." she said, though it came somewhat robotically.

I nodded. Sirens suddenly wailed in the distance and I knew someone had heard the blasts and called the police. Probably someone in the apartment house.

"Chloe," Pete said, his voice still low but shaky now. "I didn't miss him...I was aiming careful so I wouldn't hit you with any of the shot, but I know I got him. No way I could have missed..."

I took a deep breath, struggled to compose myself, because honesty I just wanted to collapse and start crying. But I couldn't, not now. I'd have to save that for later. I was just glad to be alive.

"You didn't miss..." I said, giving him a look that told him I was incredibly thankful he had come along when he did, because otherwise I would have been lying on a slab tonight and things lying on a slab in New Salem had a distressing habit of getting back up.

"It's not possible, Chloe..." he said, as if he wanted me to explain it to him, yet at the same time didn't.

Instead of saying anything further, I just went to him and gave him a hug.

Amanda remained still, looking off in the direction in which the killer had fled. Shock it was, I told myself.

Moments later, police cars, tires squealing, skidded into the parking lot and blazing blue flashes and white stabs of headlights illuminated the whole area. Men surged out of the cars and started darting about, but they left me to Johnny, who climbed out of the lead car. Johnny spent some time questioning Pete and Amanda, and I could tell from the windshield wiper change of emotions on his features, from bad to worse, he wasn't liking the answers they gave him one damn bit.

By the time he got around to me, his expression had become dark stone and I knew I was only going to make things worse.

He flipped his notebook shut and tucked it into a pocket, then took out his pack of Juicy Fruit. A moment later he was machine-gun chewing and his gaze was darting everywhere but to me. He didn't want to ask me anything about what had happened but knew he had to. It was creating a conflict within him but he was likely more than a little relieved the ripper hadn't skewered me because he would have been the one who had to inform Arly; he'd gotten a lifetime full of that back when he had had to tell him his son Bobby had been killed.

"Chloe..." he said at last, his voice trailing off, tainted with disbelief, yet with the certainty he'd stepped in a heaping pile of supernatural doody again.

I nodded, sighed. "I know, Johnny. But what can I say? You aren't going to like what I'm going to tell you."

He frowned, nodded, then gave his gum a couple more chews. "You'd think I'd be used to it."

"Tell me about it." I wrapped my arms about myself, fighting the shudders.

"You ok?" He looked at me directly for the first time, eyes filled with concern.

"I'm alive. That's a plus right now."

"You're going to have to tell Arlo about this, now."

I nodded. "I will…" *As soon as it was all over*, I added in my mind.

"Uh-huh." He didn't believe me. I wasn't that good a liar, so that was to be expected.

"It was Carlis Harlen, Johnny."

"What?" His tone dropped into a bucket of cold.

"The ripper. It was Harlen."

His brow furrowed and I think I might have seen a shiver go through him. "The hell? Harlen's dead. He hanged himself in his cell nearly a year ago. I *saw* the body."

Carlis Harlen. Remember I told you about a guy who came into the Lagoon one night who gave me the heebie jeebies? The one they caught slicing and dicing his girlfriend? That was Carlis Harlen. The same guy who had committed suicide in his cell was the same guy who had nearly shish kabobbed me half an hour ago.

"You saw Chuckles' body…"

"I wish to hell things in New Salem would just stay dead." He said it without the slightest bit of humor.

"I'll second that. They always come after me. He's one of those things that escaped. He has to be."

"Along with Lamont?"

I shook my head. "I don't know about Lamont. I think Lamont was warning me about him. I just didn't understand it. I think that's what that Mister Ed clue was, another warning. 'The source is the Devil'. Harlen was in Hell and Lamont knew I'd make the Satanic message connection sooner or later."

"In a pulling a rabbit out of your ass sort of way. So, what, now Lamont disappears? Job done?"

"I can always hope, but I have a feeling that other thing he said about unfinished business *didn't* relate to Harlen. I think that had to do with him and Marlene."

"Pete said he shot the guy twice."

"He did. Carlis took a licking and he's still ticking. Didn't have much effect other than to chase him off. But it *was* Harlen, Johnny. I got a good look at his rotted face."

"We didn't find any blood in the parking lot, either…"

"You won't, because he doesn't have any anymore. Maybe he's leaking formaldehyde..." It wasn't funny but I needed something to let a little of the pressure off.

"I'll have the forensics team check. We're going to need to rope this area off for a while. Pete agreed to close for a couple days. He's worried about his girls."

"Pete's a good guy. If not for him..."

Johnny nodded. "I'll take you and Amanda home..."

I shook my head. "No, I have my car and I was heading over to the diner for coffee with her. I need that now more than ever, and I think she does, too."

"She seems to be in shock. She didn't say much."

I glanced at the young woman, who still had a stoic look on her face, but had wrapped her arms about herself. "She's an odd one."

Sturdevant stared off into the night and I could tell things were going through his mind that were giving him a lot of problems.

"How am I going to stop him, Chlo? How am I going to stop a man who can take two shotgun blasts straight up and run away? How am I going to stop a dead man?"

"We've done it before, Johnny."

"Why doesn't that make me feel any better?" He hesitated, sighed. "I can't protect women from something like that. I can't protect *you* from it."

"I'm not asking you to. That ring might protect me. Maybe that's why Lansing had Bob give it to me. I should have had it on me tonight, then maybe I could have stopped him."

He looked at me like he didn't believe me and maybe he was right. I had been so totally frozen at seeing Harlen again he might have killed me anyway. Besides, how was I going to get a ring on his finger? Guys were notoriously difficult to pin down when it came to that, anyway.

"Arlo..."

"I know, I know. He's going to hit the ceiling because I didn't tell him any of this was going on. But please don't call him, Johnny. Let me have a little more time."

"I don't know, Chloe. Arlo originally put Harlen away, maybe he can help somehow, and if it was my wife..."

"Please? You know he'll just come running back here thinking he's going to save my ass."

"Is that such a bad thing?"

"No, not on the face of it. But I've always fended for myself and if I start relying on him too much…I'm afraid I'll lose myself and things will change between us."

"You're worried about the wind, Chloe. Things won't change. They'll only get stronger. Take it from someone who didn't trust his wife when he should have."

"A few more days…" I gave him my best puppy eyes, proving some of my nerve had come back. I had seen awful things before and I was strong, maybe stronger than he and Arly put together, the way he had told me.

He nodded. "All right, all right. Against my better judgment. Just don't get yourself cut into little pieces because Arlo would never forgive me."

"I'll be careful."

He made a *pfft* sound. "How d'you figure on doing that if you have to get a ring on Harlen's finger to send him back to wherever he came from?"

"I'll figure it out. Maybe I'll have Bob help me again."

"You really want to rely on a monkey save?"

I shook my head. "Lansing sent that monkey with the ring…" I muttered, not sure why suddenly it was bothering me.

"And Harlen shows up here…"

"You're a detective after all, Johnny. You picked right up on something I was half thinking."

He nodded. "I don't like coincidences."

"That makes two of us. Harlen was in here once, a long time ago. He hassled me then, so maybe it really is just chance he showed up here tonight. Whatever the case I'm going to have to find him."

Sturdevant's face went darker. "If he doesn't find you first…"

TWENTY-FIVE

Sweet Gypsy Marlene

"I'm sorry I froze, Chloe," Amanda Connors said, brown eyes still sad but making a good attempt at portraying guilt as well. Trouble was, I wasn't certain whether to believe her and I am not sure I could say why.

She sat across from me in a booth at the diner, her hands clamped about a mug of steaming coffee. She seemed composed enough, at least more composed than I was, for someone who had just witnessed a dead guy who'd been shot twice run away. Me, I was still shaking like a Chihuahua. I mean, even though I had seen dead guys walking around before it never got routine, you know? It still scared the living crap right out of me and I couldn't really understand how she was staying so calm. Unless she was still in shock; that was the only thing I could think of that might explain it.

Oh, excuse me, let me correct myself. Amanda Connors wasn't sitting across from me in the booth, Amanda Marlene was, at least according to Pete, and he had no reason to make it up.

I took a sip of my coffee; it was hot as hell, which explained why Amanda hadn't touched hers. I was amazed she was holding onto the mug so tightly without getting burned.

"It's ok," I said, though it wasn't, I thought. "I froze, too. I don't usually do that. I've…well, I've seen enough in my life to keep my wits about me even in the worst situations. But if it wasn't for Pete Harlen would have killed me."

"Harlen?" Her gaze drifted out through the window into the poorly lit parking lot. A few truckers sat at the counter and a handful of patrons I recognized from the Lagoon were downing pots of coffee, trying to sober up.

"Carlis Harlen. That's the name of the guy who attacked us."

She nodded, still looking out the window. "Pete shot him...twice...he ran off." She said it like it wasn't a particularly big deal, so maybe it was shock after all, but the sadness in her eyes deepened. Something else came with it, something I couldn't place.

"That might be a little hard to explain." I wasn't kidding. How do you tell somebody who hasn't been living in New Salem a dead guy was running around murdering young women? Hell, how did you tell somebody who *was* living here?

"I imagine," she said looking back to me and now I recognized what was in her eyes with the sadness: relief. Not a lot, but it was there. "I'm glad he didn't hurt you."

"I'll second that. You were lucky he didn't hurt you, either."

"I suppose I am." She looked at the table, then back up, apology on her face, which looked strangely drawn, pale. Maybe the shock was wearing off. "I couldn't have stopped him, Chloe. I'm sorry. I..." She paused, as if she wanted to say something else but couldn't. "I just couldn't have."

I touched her hand on the mug, wanting to withdraw almost immediately. Her fingers felt ice-cold again. No wonder the scalding cup wasn't bothering her. "I know you couldn't. Nobody could have, I don't think. Pete put two barrels into him and he still walked away. He would have just killed you."

"No, he didn't seem interested in me."

"I think he has a thing for blondes. He hassled me quite a while back in the Lagoon when he was..." Oh, crap, I had been about to say "when he was alive." Which would have opened a big can of worms I probably did not want to get into with her.

"When he was what?" she asked, though no real interest hung in her voice.

I decided I'd better change the subject. "Pete told me you said your last name was Marlene."

She stared at me, slight surprise registering, but remained silent.

"You introduced yourself as Connors back when we first met and on the phone yesterday..." I pushed, hoping she'd volunteer the information and I wouldn't need to press her too much after what had just occurred at the Lagoon.

She nodded. "Connors is my real name. Marlene...Marlene is a stage name. I went back to it after a few...a few guys got hold of my number."

I got the weird impression she was deliberately leaving something out, maybe even lying. "Marlene was a name around here in the '60s," I said, almost nonchalantly enough to get away with it.

She smiled, the first time I had seen her exhibit a warm emotion all night. "You don't have to skirt whatever it is you want to ask, Chloe."

I took another sip, then leaned back in the booth seat. "All right, Lillian Marlene. An actress from the early '60s. Any relation?" I expected her to lie or at least pretend she hadn't heard of the woman. To say I was surprised was putting it mildly.

Another smile. "My great aunt."

Well, color me flabbergasted. I was almost too surprised to speak. Nah, I'm never too surprised for that. "Your great aunt, the one you came back to visit, is Lillian Marlene, the actress? She's alive?" I wished I hadn't said the last part, because it was rather insensitive under the circumstances, but it just slipped out because I was stunned.

"At least for the moment. But, yes, that's her."

"I've been trying to find her, Amanda, or at least information about her. No one seems to know what happened to her after the mid-'60s."

I had slipped a little and expected her to call me on it, ask me just what my interest was in finding her aunt, and that would mean trying to explain Mr. Black and White Laughing Boy. But she didn't call me on it, and I suppose that should have made me wonder more than it did but I was a little too relieved to dwell on it.

"She had a nervous breakdown after...well, after some things happened."

"Some things such as Brant Lamont?" I leaned forward, bracing my elbows on the table.

"Him and *other* things, family things. Her career...her career was going nowhere and there was some kind of scandal. You know how it was back then. She changed her name back to Connors, Lilly Connors and bought the cottage here. People forgot about her pretty quickly. She never achieved the status worthy of being remembered other than for, well, for the suspicion of Lamont's death."

"Lamont's death? He just vanished without a trace. He could still be alive."

She shrugged. "I just assumed...well, everybody, from what I've heard, assumed he was dead."

I nodded. "Probably the most likely scenario..." I didn't want to add I knew for a fact he was amongst the dear departed, since he had visited me. Why complicate things anymore than need be?

"It's hard to believe nobody would have hounded you, especially some tabloid writer or something. Hollywood scandal books make a lot of money."

"No one has, but I was using the family name for the longest time. I just changed it to Marlene when I came here."

My brow crinkled. "Why?"

She shrugged again, drew her hands away from her coffee cup. "To honor her, I suppose, in my own way. She won't know. In fact, I don't think she would have much appreciated the idea of me stripping. It's not the side of show business she would have wanted me to get into. But soon it won't matter, will it? She'll be gone."

Sadness flooded her eyes again. I got the impression there was more to it, but maybe I was just not thinking entirely clear after all that had happened tonight. I was definitely rattled, but still...

I sighed. "You know, I can't tell you how bad I feel for you. I lost my entire family, so I understand what it's like losing somebody you care about. But I'll be honest, I also get the impression you're leaving something out. I felt it when I met you at the Coffee Shoppe yesterday and I feel it now. You can deny it, I guess, because maybe you think it isn't any of my business, but in a weird way I can't exactly explain it has become my business."

She almost smiled and that wasn't the reaction I expected. Frankly, I thought she might be a little pissed off because I was round aboutly accusing her of lying. Sorta. Well, at least of hiding something.

A distant look clouding her eyes, she gazed out the window again. "You're right. I haven't been quite honest about why I came here. To tell you the truth, I thought I was just being flaky and if I told you, you'd think I was ready for a loony bin."

I chuckled. "Try me; you'd be surprised what I'm ready to accept."

She looked back to me, nodded. "I believe you. I can see it in your eyes." She hesitated. "I didn't come here just to settle my aunt's affairs. I've been having dreams, Chloe. It's like I was drawn here...and, oh Christ, you'll think this is crazy."

"Crazy's relative," I assured her.

"I've felt like something dark has been, well, drawing me here."

Something dark? Lamont? Had he tried to contact to her, too? Why? Why would he want her here? What possible connection could she have to a missing actor? I decided to keep my encounters with him to myself for the time being but did ask:

"Tonight at the Lagoon, when I was on stage…did anything *funny* happen?"

"Funny in what way?"

I shrugged, took a sip of my coffee. "It's not important. What about your family, you have any except your great aunt? Mother? Father?" I had a small hope maybe an older relative might recall something from that early '60s period that might give me a clue to Lamont's disappearance.

"I…" A hint of confusion registered in her big brown eyes. "I don't remember them."

"You don't' remember your parents?"

"They…I think they died when I was very young. I…drifted around a lot."

I could understand that all too well. But I had been a little older when my parents were killed, so I had my memories of them. That was *all* I had.

"Have you seen her yet?" I asked, going back to the subject of her great aunt.

She shook her head. "No, I've been trying to work up the nerve."

Ok, what I asked next I asked because I genuinely wanted to help her, but I couldn't deny an ulterior motive as well. I wanted to meet Lillian Marlene, the woman who might have caused the downfall of Brant Lamont, and I had a feeling I was supposed to, that that was why he had come to me. The ripper warning, vague as it was, was probably just a perk.

"I'd like to come with you. I could pick you up."

She nodded, smiled. "I'd like that."

"Tomorrow morning, then?"

She nodded, pushed her coffee cup away. "I don't think I have the stomach for it," she said and stood. I couldn't blame her and it was getting pretty late.

I drove her to the cottage, which was about a mile and a half from the Lagoon, a fair walk, especially at night with a ripper running around. The place looked decrepit, dark, with shutters hanging off, overgrown grounds and a cracked walkway. I noticed some of the windows were still boarded over and no front porch light was on.

"This doesn't look very homey," I said, as she opened the car door and swung a leg out.

"It needs a lot of work, I suppose. Aunt Lily's been in Willow Pines a long time and nobody kept it up. I'll have to hire somebody to spruce it up before I put it on the market."

I gazed at the place again, wondering if it even had the power turned on. "The offer's still open if you want to stay with me."

She gave me a peculiar smile I couldn't read. "Thanks, Chloe, but I'll be fine. I feel…closer to her here."

I nodded, understanding, and she got out of the car, closed the door. It dawned on me, then, that I didn't see any vehicle in the driveway.

"Amanda?" I said and she leaned back in the window, shadows falling across her face.

"Yeah?"

"Where's your car?"

She hesitated. "I don't have one. I took a train in and hired a cab. I walked to the Lagoon tonight."

I nodded. "I can drive you in when Pete reopens. No more walking with that maniac on the loose."

A soft smile drifted across her lips. "Chloe…thanks…for everything."

"I'll pick you up at ten tomorrow. Try to get some sleep."

I knew sleep was too likely *not* on my own agenda tonight. I just hoped with everything that had happened Lamont gave me a break and let me shiver till sunrise in peace…

TWENTY-SIX

Lily Out of the Lamplight

Willow Pines felt like Death waiting. The air inside the building was thick and suffocating. Cloying odors of cafeteria food, urine and disinfectant permeated the gloomy hallway and large combination meeting area/dining room the desk nurse had directed us to. Amanda Marlene and I stepped onto the threadbare carpet at the room's entrance and stopped. Despite glaring arcs of sunlight that slashed through partially drawn blinds from windows on two sides, the room seemed incredibly depressing and stuffy, a place where life had passed and old dreams lay gasping on the floor.

A fireplace crackled, though it was at least 75 degrees outside, making the room unbearably hot and augmenting the amalgam of odors to the point where I wanted to breathe through my T-shirt. But it was more than just the odors and gloom; it was the creepy feeling this sort of place gave me. People came here to die. Their families, some with good intentions, some without hearts, consigned their loved ones—and I use the term loosely—to places like this when they could not, or no longer wanted to, take care of them.

It absolved them either of the responsibility of caring for them or the heartache of watching them die. No one ever left Willow Pines. Amend that: No one ever left Willow Pines breathing. Nausea clawed at my stomach and I almost wished I hadn't come. I wasn't sure what was worse, waiting for Death or actually grieving for someone departed. I didn't like either feeling one damn bit.

"There," Amanda said, voice low, the sadness on her face more pronounced, as she pointed to a wheelchair by the far window. A frail woman sat in the chair, her back to us, staring straight out.

I nodded, as comfortable in this place as I would have been in a morgue. In my opinion, there wasn't a hell of a lot of difference between the two.

We threaded our way through the tables, all of which were empty, Amanda's macramé purse bouncing at her side as she walked. I wondered where all the other residents were and the disturbing thought that maybe they had all died jumped into my mind. No, it was just early and maybe the place had a Bingo room somewhere on the premises or something. I hoped.

"Aunt Lily?" Amanda said when we reached the old woman, but no response came. Amanda touched the old woman's shoulder. Still no sign of recognition or acknowledgement that anyone was even there came from Lillian Marlene.

"Maybe she can't hear—"

Amanda shook her head. "She can hear me, she just can't respond. The last stroke took away her ability to speak. Could you, could you turn her around for me?"

I nodded with a grim expression, unable to describe the loneliness and despair crawling through me. To be all alone in a place like this, suffering, perhaps aware somewhere deep inside, yet unable to respond, make your needs known…I couldn't imagine what it must have felt like. The irrational thought of ending up this way myself if I didn't have Arly went through my mind and jangled my composure further. I had never really known my own grandparents and never had the chance to see my own parents grow old, and maybe in some weird way that was a blessing. Well, it wasn't because I lost them tragically, but you know what I mean. Sturdevant said I was stronger than he and Arly put together, and maybe in the way he meant it he had been right, but in other ways, this way, he was wrong. I wasn't strong. It was all I could do to be here, facing human mortality. It was a type of demon I was terrified to confront and felt utterly powerless against.

Of all the things that I had been through with the supernatural, all the witches, zombies, ghosts and demons I had faced, this scared the hell out of me the most, pardon the pun.

I leaned over, gripping the handles on the back of the chair and turned the old woman towards us. It was all I could do to stifle a gasp. She had to be in her 70s in my estimation, but looked in her 90s. Half her face appeared strangely frozen, which I attributed to her stroke, and wisps of gossamer white hair framed her gaunt sunken face. Half moons of darkness nested beneath her eyes, cellophanelike flesh making them look black and blue; blankness reflected from eyes covered by milky gauze. I doubted she was able to see us, or would have recognized us had she been able to. What remained of Lillian Marlene was not even a shadow of the woman whose picture I had seen on the Internet, the one vaguely reminiscent of Marilyn Monroe. This was a shell of a human being, a withered husk.

I wanted to cry. I really did. But I controlled the impulse, because Amanda didn't need me falling apart on her. Being here was hard enough on her and the sadness reflected on her face said everything I needed to know about how she was feeling. She might not have shown much in the way of emotion last night after the attack, but she did now.

I straightened, backed up a step, wrapping my arms about myself and swallowing hard. Amanda leaned in, kissed the old woman on the forehead.

"I'm here…" she said, her voice strangely distant, clashing with the emotion on her face. The old woman didn't register any expression, showed no sign of recognition.

Much of the reason I had wanted to visit Lillian Marlene was based on the remote hope I had that I could question her about Brant Lamont, but clearly that was not going to be possible. Whatever she was or had been, conniving actress or gold-digger, that woman no longer existed. She had died for all intents and purposes with the stroke.

"I brought you something." Amanda reached into her purse and pulled out a portable CD player with blue metallic cover. She set it on the old woman's lap, then turned back to me, smiling. "I was told it was her favorite song."

I nodded, wondering if the woman would even be able to enjoy it.

A chill ran through me after Amanda pressed a button and the song starting playing.

The song that came from the CD player was *Calcutta!* I should have expected it, yet it caught me completely off guard.

I wasn't the only one because for the first time the old woman showed a response and it wasn't a good one. Noises came from somewhere deep within her throat, gurgling, yet high-pitched, almost as if the song caused her some sort of pain. Amanda watched her, frozen for a minute, and I assumed too shocked to shut the thing off. I was nearly paralyzed myself but suddenly stepped forward and jabbed the stop button.

The old woman ceased making noises, for which I was immensely relieved, because the sound had been unnerving, pitiful.

Amanda straightened, tucked the player back into her purse. "I don't understand it. I thought she would like it."

"Who told you it was her favorite song?" I asked for lack of a better question. I was still trying to compose myself.

"Why...I don't know. No one told me, I guess. I just knew it or heard it somewhere growing up that she had liked this song."

I looked at the old woman, whose expression still retained its normal paralyzed appearance. No, she hadn't liked that song. Not at all. And I had a feeling there was a damn good reason for that, though at this juncture I had no clue what that reason might be.

Amanda leaned down again, gripping both arms of the chair. "Please, I'm sorry. I thought you would like it."

Aunt Lily didn't show the least little sign of acknowledgment she had heard Amanda, though if she had heard the music something inside her was at least partially aware. Whatever it was about that song, it had been the only thing strong enough to penetrate the gray haze of her mind and cause a response.

I touched Amanda's shoulder. "Perhaps we should go." I honestly don't know if I said it for her benefit or my own, but I do know I had no desire to spend even another minute in the nursing home.

TWENTY-SEVEN

Matters of Life and Death

Nobody wants to die. It frightens us, the great unknown of death, the question of whether something better exists beyond this world, beyond the veil. I believe there has to be something better because I've seen the things that slithered across the border between Hell and Earth. But most people did not have that advantage, if you could call it that, and despite their religious beliefs many deep down inside felt what happens after we depart still came down to a crapshoot. Was Heaven merely a fairytale fabricated to comfort us and relieve our fear of passing? Or was it a grand reward for the all the crap we suffered through on this earth, all the pain and loss, the disappointments?

That was a question for deeper thinkers than myself, and I am not ashamed to admit it. But I believed in something, and not just because of the things I had seen, but because not to believe meant those I had lost, my parents, perhaps my sister, had simply ceased to be and I could not face that. I had enough trouble just dealing with the fact I would never see them again in this world, my parents at least, because I still clung to a desperate hope I would find my sister alive.

But I think the true fear for most of us isn't really death; it's dying, suffering on the way out. It's a fear of pain, and of turning into what I had seen had become of Lillian Marlene. She was a woman only vital in old movies. She could not longer speak or relate, nor feel the pleasures she had felt when she was young. Even the simplest things life had to offer, a soft breeze, a lover's caress, eluded her. She was a prisoner in her own body. Was that prison worse for a woman whose very existence was based on the gratification she took from her image, the accolades granted by fame, even fame never fully realized because

Fate had stepped in and dealt her a bad hand, deserved or unwarranted?

As a stripper I could relate to that aspect of her life somewhat. Self-worth was fragile, a house of cards, and I damn well knew that. But I was lucky, because I had found someone who gave me reason to reassess what made me a person, and that was not my looks and the fact I was genetically blessed enough make a living out of that gift. Lillian Marlene had not been that lucky, had she? I wondered. Had she been nothing more than a shallow façade of a woman who used an older man for personal gain? Had she never known love with him, only ambition? Is that why Lamont had come back, for some kind of revenge? If so, he was too late; karma had beaten him to it. Or was I misjudging her? Was there more to it, and to Lamont's reason for returning now, with Marlene so close to death?

I wasn't certain at this point, but seeing her brought my recent questioning of my career to a head. It told me I questioned myself for all the right reasons, not because I was worried about getting older and losing what made me worth something; namely, my body and looks and stripping career, but because the thing that made life bearable, made a person complete, was learning how to care and sacrifice for another, to love another more than one's self. Arly had given me that, and I had given it to him. Either of us would have died for the other.

Lillian Marlene? Maybe she had died for herself. I didn't know. But I wanted to find out.

As I drove back through the waterfront after dropping Amanda at her cottage, my body and mind felt incredibly heavy, my heart leaden. I wasn't usually this despondent or philosophical but seeing that old woman's condition had done something to me and I had a feeling it wasn't totally coming from within.

"Lamont..." I whispered, turning onto a narrow side street that led to the theater district, such as it was. He didn't respond, and the world didn't flash to black and white, but I had half-expected it to.

I focused on the old buildings before me, determined whatever Lamont wanted from me wasn't going to drag me down. And with Harlen running around holding a blade with my name on it I couldn't allow myself to get too distracted by depression.

I was strong. Sturdevant had said so.

I just needed to accept that.

I just wish I didn't feel like bawling my eyes out.

TWENTY-EIGHT

Johnny on the Spot

It took me about fifteen minutes to find a parking space, then another five to parallel park because I screwed it up six times, much to the irritation of a driver in the car behind me. Some chicklet on a cell phone, who could consider herself lucky I wasn't in the mood to teach her just what a stripper cougar could do to a bitch kitty who got on her nerves. The young ones nowadays figured everything revolved around them but they had some harsh life lessons in their future. I was suddenly glad I'd never had kids.

For the most part, the buildings in this section of town were a century or more old, but the New Salem Theater, started in 1960 and completed near the end of '61 was considerably more modern, though still dated on its façade. A poster behind glass advertised a production of *Mamma Mia* starting in two weeks and the place barely kept itself supported, most of that coming by way of generous donations from some of the town's bigwigs. I only knew that because of Johnny, which reminded me...

I pulled my cell phone out of my backpack and hit the button for his programmed number. He picked up after three rings, still sighing.

"You knew it was me, I take it?" I said, a slight laugh in my voice.

"Caller ID, modern marvel," he said, tone reserved, waiting for the other shoe to drop.

"I'm not feeling the love here, Johnny. I need a favor."

"Nothing supernatural?"

"Not directly." I heard relief flood his voice and an exhalation that probably blew papers off his desk.

"You still good with that woman you dated who managed the New Salem Theater?"

"I see her from time to time. She hasn't castrated me or anything yet."

"You say that like it was a common occurrence."

"I'm not easy on the women I date since…well, since my divorce. No one ever seems to live up to…you know."

"I know. I just need for you to call her and have her let me wander around the theater for a little while."

"I guess I don't really have to ask why. Lamont?"

"You got it."

"What do you hope to find in the theater?"

That was a good question, and the answer was likely the reason Amanda had given me for coming to New Salem: I felt compelled to come here to take a look inside, as if Lamont wanted me to do it and that explained some of my sudden depression. He was getting stronger, I think, reaching out for me more, but for what reason still wasn't clear. I truly feel he was warning me about Harlen, though not directly—you know, I'm always complaining about how Evil doesn't dial direct, but Good isn't a hell of a lot better. It never came right out with anything, either. Which maybe meant Lansing was on the right side after all.

"I don't know what I hope to find, Johnny," I said at last. "Maybe nothing, but Lamont wants something out of me and the more I think about it the more convinced I am he didn't escape from Hell when Arly killed Ficatier. Maybe he's just been in stasis and something activated his ghost. I'm not sure what, but I think he's going to lead me to the answer eventually."

"Or to your death."

Well, there was that.

"Any sign of Harlen?"

"Nothing yet, but you didn't really expect there would be, did you?"

"No, I guess I didn't. I was hoping to put that ring to use, though."

"That strike you as too easy?"

"The ring?"

"Yeah, I mean, a monkey did give it to you."

"He gave me the locket, too. If I could get hold of little Ms. Pixie Sticks I might be able to get some answers on that."

"Or not. She's evasive to say the least."

"She's an A-1 bitch, as far as I'm concerned but until I know her motives and just who she is…and she did help Arly with the Sisters."

"Helped him or gave him the implement to open that hell door?" He had enough cynicism in his tone for both of us.

"Half empty, half full…"

"Dirty water either way, I'm thinking. I'll make a call."

"I'm in front of the theater now…"

I hung up and stuffed the phone in its pouch, then leaned back on the seat and waited, giving Johnny time to get hold of her. A voice of common sense coming from somewhere deep in my mind, urged me just to start the car, drive home and crawl under the blankets for the rest of the day.

I did what I usually do: I ignored it.

TWENTY-NINE

A Day at the Theater

I must have been more emotionally and physically exhausted than I thought because the sound of my cell going off woke me up and the glaring sun coming through the car windshield stung my eyes. After fishing the phone out of my backpack, I mumbled a hello and it was Johnny telling me he had gotten hold of his sometimes date and it was perfectly ok for me to take a tour of the New Salem Theater, just don't touch anything.

What was I, two? Or maybe his date was just a little annoyed at him helping a stripper friend. Hard to tell with women, sometimes, and I was one.

Grabbing my backpack after I hung up and stowed my phone, I got out of my car and stood on the sidewalk, staring at the recessed doorway leading into the theater. The double doors were dark, the glass tinted to keep tourists from peering in, probably. I went to them, grabbed one of the brass bar handles and pushed. It was unlocked and when I stepped into the lobby I saw a dark-haired woman with glasses and penciled eyebrows in her '30s giving me a look that instantly told me she was the one whom Johnny had dated. The look assessed me, not finding a lot to like if the tiniest curl of her lip were any indication.

"I'm engaged," I said, feeling like I had to explain myself for some weird reason. "Johnny is a friend of my fiancée's."

She nodded and her attitude softened a bit, though her face was still kind of sharp and hard. I guessed that was her usual look. She was a theater type, after all.

"John said you wanted to look around…"

It was an open-ended statement, of course, and she wanted to know why, but I had no desire to tell her I was hoping find a connection to a ghost.

"I'm…doing some research…" I said, not really lying but not really telling the truth, either.

"May I ask for what?"

Well, damn, this one wasn't going to be easily put off, was she?

"You can ask." I said it like it was supposed to be a funny but she was not amused. "Article for…um, a school paper."

Well, that sounded just retarded and instantly the cold look swept back onto her face. Her eyes said, You're too damn old to be a student. I wondered if I should be insulted.

"Be quick about it, we've got our hands full with *Mamma Mia* coming in."

I nodded, and she wandered off somewhere. I stood in the lobby, gazing over the arched ceiling and walls filled with posters spanning back more than forty years. Oddly enough I didn't see any for *Sliver of Darkness*, but I bet that was a part of their history they preferred to forget.

The main room was blocked by carved wooden doors a good ten feet high. I opened one and stepped into the auditorium. A foot-worn carpet lined the aisles between rows of padded velvet seats. A mezzanine and second balcony appeared dark and shadowy. Deep blue velvet curtains covered a stage adorned with large potted pants on either side. A door to the left of the stage led to the back. An eerie feeling washed over me in here, and I could swear I almost heard whispers echoing through time.

It felt like I had just stepped into *Phantom of the Opera* or something.

"Christine…" I said, just to see how my voice would carry.

I'd never been to the theater. I'd broached it once or twice to Arly but his taste ran more to baseball games and the Lagoon, so the thought of attending a play made him a little wiggly. But a lot of the old movies I watched made it look glamorous and I'd sometimes imagined myself in a sequined gown and Arly in a tux…

Arly in a tux. I laughed aloud. Yeah, right. Keep dreaming, I told myself, and took a few steps down the sloping aisle.

The closer I got to the stage the stronger the eerie depressive feeling became. It was as if something were in here with me, something lurking in the shadows. The room held barely any light, only a couple small wall lamps turned low on either side. Despite the carpeting, each step I took carried a slight echo.

Chloe…

Ok, now did I imagine I had just heard my name whispered? I'm thinking, no. Butterflies of fear started fluttering in my belly.

"Lamont?" I said, my voice coming out lower than I wanted it to.

He didn't answer and I breathed sigh of relief, though I am not sure why, because after all I had come here to see him.

Help me…

Ok, now I *know* I heard that. I stood stock still, gazing around. I swore shadows moved in every frickin' corner. My heart started going bangedy-bang-bang and a chilled sensation slithered across my lower back.

"Where are you?" I said, my voice no stronger and but my urge to run increasing exponentially. "Lamont? Is that you?"

I suddenly wondered if the woman who'd let me in could hear me because explaining who I was talking to might be problematic.

"You wanted me here," I said. "Why? Why call me here, then hide?"

What was I, stupid? I should have known better than to ask that because suddenly the world went black and white again.

THIRTY

Past, Present and Never to Be

Everything stood out in stark relief, the seats, the plants, the stage, all in black and white. But somehow the room looked different and it took me a minute to figure out how. Then it hit me: the curtain was open and to the left side of the stage there was no door, now, just an unfinished area piled with bricks and a recess in the wall. As if I had stepped back in time to the unfinished theater of 1961. A small blue plastic radio rested on the right corner of the stage, playing low, *Wonderland by Night* by Bert Kaempfert, an announcer said, as the song ended and Roy Orbison's *Crying* came from the speaker a few seconds later.

"Jesus, Marl, what do you expect me to do?" a voice crashed out and I started, big time. I turned my head towards center stage and suddenly two people stood there, each holding a script. The man had spoken and I could not clearly see his shadowed features but I knew it was Lamont. He wore the cape and slouch hat. In front of him stood a young woman, her Marilyn Monroe looks unmistakably those of Lillian Marlene. Anger twisted her face into something south of beautiful and she turned from him, then stomped down the small steps leading off the left side of the stage.

"Where the hell are you going?" he yelled and she stopped, spun, glaring.

"I expect you to do the right thing, Brant. Divorce her."

He sighed, shucked the hat and tossed it to the stage floor. He dropped his script atop it, then came down the stairs and stood before her again. "You know better than that. If this gets out…"

"If this gets out?" The woman's eyes flamed. They didn't seem to be aware of my presence, because Lamont looked right in my direction and made absolutely no acknowledgement of my being there. "How the hell do you think I'm going to hide it exactly, Brant?"

"The studio will take care of it, you can go somewhere—"

"Like they took care of that incident you had with Jacobs that got you blackballed?"

"What was I s'posed to do? He owned the goddamn studio, Marl. He was a powerful man."

"And a goddamn fruit."

"I couldn't give him what he wanted."

"So he ruined your career. I've heard the sob story a hundred times but I have to wonder if maybe you aren't the actor, after all. Maybe you just made the whole thing up because you're a has-been."

He slapped her, then. The crack reverberated throughout the room and time. She didn't cry, barely even flinched but balls of muscle stood out on either side of her jaw. Fury glinted in her eyes.

"You sonofabitch!" she screeched. "You goddamned sonofabitch!" She charged him, and her small fists beat against his chest. To his credit, he stood there and took it until she wore herself out.

"You don't really have much to complain about, do you?" he said. "You wanted a career, now you've got one. You think I didn't know you were using me?"

"You're wrong, Brant. At first I thought about it. I really did. I thought I would use you for whatever I could get out of you." She was either a good actor or meant it, I wasn't sure which, but sincerity rang in her words. Which meant she had been lying to the detective when he questioned her about Brant Lamont's disappearance. She knew he wasn't gay.

He laughed, an arrogant thing that sent fingernails of annoyance along my nerves. "That's why you spread your legs, isn't it, honey?"

His tone was enough to piss off a monk and got him a return slap. His head rocked and blood trickled from his lip.

"You filth," she said, voice lowering and freezing over.

He shrugged. "You used me, I used you, now we go our separate ways. I have big options coming up, Marl. You can't be a part of them, not the way—"

"That's all you give a damn about, isn't it, Brant? Your goddamn precious career!"

He laughed again, not quite as arrogant this time. "Isn't that what *you* cared about? Isn't that why you sought me out, like all those other young women hoping to escape their small little lives?"

"Like I said, maybe at first. Maybe I did. But things changed. I actually goddamn fell in love with you."

Another laugh and I could tell that one hurt her because her expression went dead and her eyes got the look of a corpse. "You have a school girl crush, Marl. There's plenty of other actors you can screw your way to the top with."

He turned and began to walk towards me. Tears rushed from her eyes and she sank to her knees, next to a pile of bricks littering the side of the stage. From the radio came the opening notes of *Calcutta*...

Then she was gone. Just like that, and Lamont wasn't in front of me anymore, either. He sat in one of the chairs to my left, the cape draped over his shoulders and his features nearly clear now.

"I'm not strong enough to show you the rest yet..." he said, and this time I knew he was talking to me.

"What do you want?" I asked, not sure what to say.

"Your help, Chloe." He said my name as if he had known me all his life. He'd seen me naked, though, so I guess maybe that made us family.

He peered at me and I could see his eyes now, his angular features. "I was an arrogant sonofabitch. Marl was right, I didn't care about anyone or anything but getting my career back, being a somebody after what happened..."

"What *did* happen, Lamont? Rumors said the studio was covering your..."

"Homosexuality?" He uttered a thin laugh, derisive, bitter. "The studio head was a man of particular tastes, to be certain."

So that explained it. He'd scorned a man in a position of power. "So you were never..."

"No. I...loved Marl...in my way..."

"That's not the way it looked from what I just saw." It should have really dawned on me I was standing here talking to a ghost but for some reason I no longer felt particularly afraid of him. What I saw now looked more like a beaten-down man, one who'd spent too much time contemplating his own failings.

"What it looked like and what it was are two different things. I didn't realize it at the time."

"She's dying, you know…"

His eyes took on the same sadness I had seen I Amanda's. "I know."

"Why come to me? Why now?"

"Because you can help. Only a few people can be reached on this plain. As for why now…that's because she has—"

He vanished. Just gone, and the world suddenly flooded with color. The bricks and unfinished doorway disappeared and the curtain was again closed. Getting the feeling of eyes boring into me, non-ghostly eyes, I spun, and standing in the doorway, her arms crossed and her face cemented with a decidedly unpleasant look was Sturdevant's sometimes date.

"Who were you talking to?" she asked and it wasn't a maybe. She had heard me, but had she seen Lamont?

"I was, uh…" Anything I said was going to sound crazy if she hadn't seen him, wasn't it? "What color was the room when you came in here?" I countered.

Her penciled eyebrow arched, telling me exactly what I wanted to know. She hadn't seen any black and white ghost world.

"Was anyone else here when you came up, sitting in that seat?" I ducked my chin towards where Lamont had been sitting, but I knew it was pretty much a useless question.

"I think you should leave," she said and by her tone it wasn't up for debate.

I nodded, sighed and started up the aisle. "Eye pencil is so '60s…" I muttered, feeling a little catty.

"You should tell Johnny not to send anyone else here…" she said and I frowned. I couldn't blame her. Had I seen someone standing there talking to themself I might have reacted the same way.

I bet Johnny was going to hear about it, too, and might not be getting anymore dates with Miss Manager, but maybe I was doing him a favor. She was kind of a bitch.

THIRTY-ONE

The More You Learn the Less You Know

I sat on my sectional, nursing a cup of decaf and staring out into the shadowy night beyond my patio. I'd spent a lot of the day replaying my encounter with Brant Lamont's ghost at the theater. Despite being interrupted, I think he had given me enough information to start putting some of the puzzle pieces together. I had witnessed what was likely Lamont and Marlene's final encounter, their last argument, because later that night something had happened to him. He had walked off the face of the earth, perished, either by his own hand, or someone else's.

Obviously, Marlene had started out as a gold-digger, someone looking to further her career, but the passion in her voice during their argument...the more I thought about it the more I figured that couldn't be faked. She had loved him and therein lay the problem. Something happened between them, something that would need covering by the studio. Something Lamont wanted no part of.

She'd lied to the police the night of his disappearance, furthered the rumor he was a closet homosexual. Why? Because she was protecting someone, the answer came back. But who? Herself? Him?

And what about Lamont? Did he love her? Maybe he hadn't realized it at the time, but I think he did. I think he knew it now, and that's partly why he was back. But there had to be another reason he had returned after all this time. Something had drawn him out, and it all centered, in my opinion, around Marlene's impending death. I wasn't the detective; Arly was, but I would have bet him on this one.

The song had upset her; the song had been playing at the theater right before Lamont vanished. Maybe *Calcutta* had simply triggered some dim memory of that night in 1961 when the actor walked out on her.

So why had he come to me? Why did he need my help? Ok, I was a magnet for the supernatural and not everybody could see his type. So was Arly, but Arly was out of town. Maybe Lamont would have haunted *him* had he been here. Lucky me. Yay.

A slight noise from outside interrupted my thoughts and my gaze focused back on the patio. It had sounded like the scuff of a foot but I saw nothing out there but shifting shadows caused by the breeze rustling through some of the trees lining the property. I shivered, despite myself, my nerves still jumpy from the attack last night.

Where was I? Oh, yeah. Lamont and Marlene.

And what about Amanda? Marlene's great niece. Another coincidence? I think not. Amanda claimed she had felt drawn here by something dark. Had that been Lamont calling to her? Why? Of what use would she be to him? I still couldn't make a connection.

Yet, Amanda hid some secret, that was plain; she wasn't telling me something, so maybe she had lied about the darkness calling her here. Ugh, I was confusing myself.

Then there was Bob and Ms. Lansing and a certain ring. But the ring had nothing to do with Lamont, as far as I could see. The ring had something to do with Harlen, and perhaps like the locket it was a protection charm or something with which to send the killer back to Hell.

Jack the Ripper. The book on Lansing's desk. What did Jack the ripper have to do with Harlen? Or was that just Lansing's private little joke left for me because she knew sooner or later I was going to come barging in there and give her holy hell for yet another monkey visit? She was on my list, that's for sure.

Lamont had warned me about Harlen, in his way. I was sure of that. *Mister Ed* and whispered words. Why? Was he trying to atone for the way he had been in life? Did he want to keep me alive long enough to help him with whatever it was he needed me for? Or had his TV/play character somehow just melded itself to his spirit, caused him to intervene out of some weird sense of manufactured fictional justice?

I felt certain this time I was dealing with two disparate manifestations, one of them searching for something, the other malicious, one of Hell's escapees.

"One at a time," I whispered, then took a sip of my coffee.

I nearly spilled it all over my robe when the phone rang.

THIRTY-TWO

When Johnny Calls

I was really starting to have this thing about phones. I was getting so I hated them ringing, especially when I was alone at night in my apartment and supernatural boos were chasing me. Phones that rang at night were never good news in my experience, but coming on the heels of ghosts and escapee hellnicks they were even worse omens and always jangled my already jumpy nerves.

I set my cup on the coffee table next to my *Night Demons* book, which I still hadn't finished reading because I had sort of lost my taste for horror after living it the past few weeks, and checked the caller ID. I let out a breath of relief and picked up the phone.

"Hey, Chlo," John Sturdevant said, less apprehension in his voice than normal.

"This is a switch. Usually I'm the one calling you."

He laughed and I stood, started pacing a little, still agitated.

"I got a weird call from Jenny Marples."

"Who now?"

"You met her today at the theater."

"Oh. Her." I had a feeling I knew where this was going.

"Yeah, she seems to think you have issues."

"Not like I could debate that with her, but those theater types aren't exactly low on the neurotic scale, either."

"She wasn't real happy with me."

"She's no good for you anyway." I tried to make it a joke, but he didn't find it funny. I could tell.

"Anyway, she said you were talking to yourself."

"I was talking to Lamont."

"I figured. That's why I called. I found some info on him. The studio head he had the fight with—"

"Was gay, I know."

"Well, that just busted my bubble."

"Sorry, Johnny. I put it together from what Lamont and Marlene were arguing about and what Lamont told me. The studio head was gay and wanted more from Lamont than he was willing to give so he blackballed him for not giving in. Lamont struggled until he got that *Sliver of Darkness* part, then the play, but had some pretty hot irons in the fire as you said, the Bond franchise and all that. He planned to be big again."

"So Marlene wanted to ride his coattails?" I could hear him unwrapping something, probably a stick of Juicy Fruit because a few seconds later he was chewing in my ear.

"Not exactly. I think originally she set out to sleep her way up, but fell in love with him. Something happened after that, and Lamont left her, then vanished."

"Something?"

"I'm not sure exactly what, but Lamont said he needed my help."

"For what?"

"Still on my to-find-out list."

"Here's something you probably don't have…"

"Amanda Connors is Lillian Marlene's great niece. Lillian Connors is in a nursing home called Willows Pines."

Heavy sigh. Really heavy. I should learn to keep my mouth shut and stroke his ego a bit more, since he goes out of his way to help me so much.

"Crap, Chloe, you told me you weren't the detective."

"I got lucky. I went to see Marlene with Amanda earlier today."

"She have anything to say?"

"Couldn't, she's virtually a vegetable."

"There's something else."

"Ok, you got me on this one, Johnny." I think I heard him smile.

"Amanda Connors, I couldn't find any record for her. She gave me the Marlene name last night when I questioned her but I wanted to check it out before mentioning it to you. I wasn't sure she was Lillian's grand niece until you just told me, only that there had to be a relation because Lily Connors came up in a search of nursing home databases."

"Amanda moved around a lot but they were originally from New York, I think."

"I know. Nanuet, New York. I ran a check on Lillian and I found a few relatives left, but none under the name Amanda Connors or Amanda Marlene."

"Maybe she changed her first name, too?"

"Could be."

I was about to say something but the words stuck in my throat. I had chanced looking out onto the patio and for a heartbeat I thought I glimpsed shadowy movement, but it just as quickly vanished, so I couldn't be sure.

"Chloe?" Sturdevant's voice came with a note of worry.

"I...I'm here..." My voice trembled and I realized I was still really wound up from last night's encounter with Harlen. I stared out at the patio, not really wanting to see anything, but at the same time needing to make certain I hadn't.

"What's wrong?" Sturdevant asked, the worry growing stronger.

"Nothing, I guess. I think my nerves are getting the better of me. I thought I saw something outside on my patio, but it was probably the shadow of a branch."

"All the same, I'm sending a man over to watch your place. I'd feel better and I *know* Arlo would."

"I won't argue with you, Johnny."

"There's the real switch."

I hung up, more glad than I could have told him that someone would be watching my place tonight. Maybe I'd actually be able to get some sleep.

I watched the patio for a few moments, telling myself I had seen nothing, then stared at the pipe in the slider door and weighed the scales on which was safer, the pipe staying where it was to prevent someone from breaking in—supernatural boos who took shotgun blasts were probably strong enough to bust through the glass any-way—or grabbing the pipe and sleeping with it tonight. The second option won. I went to the slider, worried that something would jump up outside like in those cheesy horror movies and scare the piss out of me, grabbed the pipe and scrambled back. Nothing jumped but you couldn't have guessed it by looking at me. I was scared. I wanted to call Arly before going to bed, but I knew if I did he would hear the worry in my voice and come running back. So I forced myself to turn off the lights and go upstairs, pipe in one hand, a mythical set in the other.

THIRTY-THREE

Goosebumps in the Night

3:30am

I sat at my vanity table, studying the ring Bob had left me. I'd
pinned my hair up in a bun and wore an oversized T-shirt, because I
was not going to be sleeping without clothes until this whole Lamont
and ripper thing was over with. Being caught naked for two nocturnal
invasions were quite enough, thank you. Plus Sturdevant's cop was
patrolling outside keeping an eye on the place, so if he wanted a show
he'd have to go to the Lagoon and pay for it like everybody else.

I opened the center drawer and rummaged through the hairbrushes,
hair ties and various other do-dads a woman couldn't live without until
I located a thin silver chain. I shoved the drawer shut, then threaded
the ring onto the chain and closed the clasp. After draping it around
my neck I stared at its reflection in the mirror. I wasn't going to be
caught without it this time if Harlen showed up, and I still wasn't entirely certain I hadn't seen some sort of shadowy movement on my
patio that amounted to more than swaying branches. The last time I
had faced a demon, Bob, or Lansing, take your pick, had given me my
sister's old locket as a protection device, one that ultimately destroyed
Praetallious. Although the ring kind of creeped me out, what with the
Devil face embedded into its black stone that made it hard to believe it
was anything beneficial, I had no reason to assume it was anything different from the locket. In theory, anyway. However, I was basing everything on an assumption and the word—if you could call it that—of a
monkey.

All right, so Bob hadn't actually *told* me it was for my protection, but he had brought me the locket and that all turned out just peachy. So why did I have this king-sized knot in my stomach?

Because you don't trust Lansing, a voice deep in my mind returned.

I frowned. Again I considered calling Arly, but told myself I just wasn't a good enough liar to conceal the fear I was experiencing; he would hear it in my voice and come running back to New Salem. We were a couple, and we had faced a lot of supernatural crap together but I was still my own woman and sometimes stubborn to a fault.

I glanced back over a shoulder, seeing Puddin' Head had taken up his usual spot on the end of my bed. I was getting the hairy cat eye for keeping him up past his bedtime. I'd sat here for the past hour, thinking over Lamont and Harlen and everything that had happened and had no desire to turn the lights off, which apparently pissed off the hairy masses no end.

"All right, all right," I muttered. He did have a point. It *was* late and I couldn't avoid the dark forever.

With a sigh, I switched off the vanity track lights and stood, waiting for my eyes to adjust to the darkness. Moonlight blazed through the windows but was not the least bit comforting.

My nerves made my stomach a little nauseated and I swore the shakes had moved into my body permanently. I was safe in my home with that cop patrolling outside, right? Against a killer who took two blasts from a shotgun? another voice asked. Against a ghost who turned my world black and white and showed up inside my townhouse in the dead of night?

Ok, I wasn't helping myself any. Harlen didn't know where I lived, anyway. I hoped.

He's Evil, he doesn't need Mapquest.

Yeah, there was that.

Crap on a cracker.

I did have my pipe. Ok, that was a plus. And an attack cat. I glanced at Puddin' Head, who was a good ten or maybe even twenty pounds overweight. Scratch that last one, I thought. He'd be lucky to get out of his own way.

This was useless. I was just scaring myself worse and Lamont wasn't a threat, as far as I could tell. He had tried to warn me. Harlen...Harlen was a threat but he stalked the waterfront. His being in the back parking lot might have just been a coincidence. Right? He wasn't targeting me specifically.

And I had the ring. The shadow on my patio had been tree branches.

Ok. Now I was cool.

Pretty much.

I made a sudden dash for my bed and burrowed under the covers. Ok, not so much, but what choice did I have? I grabbed the pipe I'd stashed under the opposite pillow, its cold thickness comforting. Undead or not, I could still brain the sonofabitch.

I was dead tired, but I had the feeling I wasn't going to sleep. I had the feeling a whole lot stronger half an hour later after I'd lain there in the dark staring at the ceiling, my mind racing and my heart not far behind. Apparently, Puddin' Head had no such issues, because the furry little butthead was fast asleep and snoring his ass off.

I should have called Arly. I shouldn't have been so stubborn. Don't be silly, I chastised myself, he couldn't have gotten here tonight, anyway, and I'd still be lying here worried about every little sound coming from outside. I suddenly hated crickets, by the way. They made entirely too much noise.

A sound.

My heart jumped into my throat and my hand clasped the pipe so tight my fingers ached.

This time I had heard a noise and it was no cricket or one of the normal night sounds filtering through the open window. A bump of some kind, though I wasn't entirely sure where it had come from.

I sat up in bed, stared at my closed bedroom door. The world did not turn black and white, so I was fairly sure Lamont wasn't making one of his nocturnal visits.

I listened but the sound of my heart thudding and my pulse throbbing in my ears made it hard to hear any outside sounds.

Another bump and I nearly jumped off the bed. I posied on the edge, blanket twisted around my bare legs, the pipe clutched before my chest.

Downstairs. Dammit! The sound had come from downstairs.

"Where's your cop, Johnny?" I whispered, knowing one cop was pretty useless against Harlen if he had somehow found me.

Evil knows where you live.

The thought didn't help my composure any. I forced myself to stand, legs feeling like they wanted to go in two different directions, shaking. It was all I could do to keep my balance.

You're braver than this, I told myself. You faced the Sisters of the Snake and Praetallious and you have that ring around your neck.

That was better. I had my pipe, too. Yes I did.

Keep telling yourself that, girl. Don't let a bump freeze you.

The way you froze with Harlen last time he attacked?

I couldn't do that again. Pete wasn't here to save me. But last time seeing a dead man was a shock. This time I expected him. This time I had a frickin' pipe.

Wait a minute, it was just a bump, well, two bumps, downstairs. Nobody said it had to be a psycho hellkiller, right? There might be some perfectly logical...

Nah. I knew better. My stripper sense was tingling to the point of making me want to climb out the second story window and take my chances dropping to the ground. One bump was possible to explain away, two was a psycho hellkiller, I just knew it.

I drew a deep breath, summoned every bit of nerve I had left, then walked to my bedroom door and gripped the handle with my left hand. With my right I lifted the pipe, ready to brain anyone who might be standing on the other side. If it was Harlen he wasn't going to catch me freezing this time. I wasn't some little tweak in a horror movie. I'd been through Hell and back.

The handle felt cool but not filmy, the way it had when Lamont appeared. I clasped it, my knuckles bone-white in the moonlight, then pulled open the door...

THIRTY-FOUR

Guns Don't Kill People, Psycho Hellkillers Do

I wanted to scream, nevermind the fact that when I opened the door no one was standing in the hallway. Every fear inside me had just built up like a teakettle ready to toot and wanted to release itself in one big mother of a screech. I managed to choke it back and not completely alert whoever was in the house, if indeed somebody was, I was awake and ready for them with my trusty pipe.

Holding onto the pipe like it was the last blouse at a 50 percent off sale, I stared out into the shadowy hallway, wishing I could swallow my thumping heart. My legs felt syrupy and I thought for a moment I was going to collapse. The cat was still snoring away behind me. Note to self: Get a dog. A really big dog.

I forced myself out into the hallway, ears pricked for any sounds coming from the downstairs level but nothing except for the sound of my own body functions in high panic mode thrummed in my ears. I swallowed, lowered my pipe to my chest and took a couple more steps.

It dawned on me that maybe I should call Sturdevant before trying to confront whatever was awaiting me and I instantly found myself backing up into my room. I padded to the nightstand, lifted the phone as if any little noise it would make would send a psycho hellkiller charging up the stairs and into my room. I hesitated, worrying the moment I hit the button the dial tone might be loud enough to be heard from below. Just in case, I set my pipe on the bed and grabbed a pillow, putting it over the receiver when I pressed the button.

It was a useless gesture. Because no dial tone came from the thing and I knew that was a damn poor sign. I just couldn't win with phones.

They were trouble when they worked and trouble when they didn't. Wasn't it bad enough I was doing the stupid girl in a horror movie routine again by going downstairs to confront a psycho hellkiller without adding the clichéd dead phone routine?

But it wasn't so formula when it really happened to you. It was frickin' unnerving.

I dropped the phone and grabbed my pipe again. For the second time I glanced at the window with the half-assed thought of jumping out. That would be good for a broken leg at the least, wouldn't it? Then I'd be a sitting duck.

I forced myself to go back out into the hall, not liking my options one damn bit. My stomach did a cartwheel and I think I threw up a little in my mouth. Yum.

Crap, crap, crap. Why couldn't I have just had a simple life without boos showing up that wanted to kill me or use my soul for some dark purpose? Didn't the Big Weird have anything better to do than pick on strippers?

Holding my breath, I reached the top of stairs and stared down. Nothing moved at the bottom and that only brought a modicum of relief. I allowed myself a deep breath and took the first step as quietly as I could, but my legs weren't working right and I thumped down a little harder than I expected. I held my breath again. Waited.

Nothing. Either my step hadn't been heard or was being ignored.

I got a sudden urge to yell to whatever was below and just get the shock of it jumping out at me over with. Only the most tenuous of holds on my good judgment kept me from doing something that idiotic.

I eased down another few steps, barely able to make myself breathe, getting light headed; little sparkly lights danced before my vision. I forced myself to take a bigger breath before I ended up passing out and toppling down the stairs.

It might have been an animal running into the slider door, I tried to tell myself, knowing better. Yeah, well, did that same animal cut the phone line?

Ok, had me there. It wasn't an animal.

You know what it is.

I knew. Harlen. He was here. Something about me had either stuck in his brain from that time at the Lagoon or Evil had sent him after me on purpose. It didn't really matter because I knew that's who it was below, waiting, lurking, lusting for blood.

My pipe wasn't going to be enough to protect me. Maybe nothing could.

The ring...

I had that, didn't I? That had to be it. That had to be the answer, just like with Praetallious and the locket. My fingers went to it; it felt cold, not the least bit comforting.

Slightly emboldened by my decree I went down the rest of the way. At the bottom I paused, eyes scanning the lower level, slices of moonlight serrating the carpet and blending with shards of shadow. Darkness clogged every corner, cloistered behind the counter and the sectional couch.

I looked towards the slider doors and that scream I had wanted to let loose upstairs clawed its way up my throat again.

THIRTY-FIVE

Rippers and Strippers, Oh My!

I don't know how I held onto that scream; I really don't. I wanted to just shriek my freakin' lungs out. But I didn't.

The slider door was open. Wide open, and it made me suddenly debate my earlier logic about removing the pipe. Of course, then maybe whoever had forced it might have just busted through the glass and I would be standing here weaponless, so maybe I had made the right choice after all.

It took only a half minute to make myself move, but it felt like an eternity. I eased down the three steps leading to the sunken living room, pipe held high, heart banging against my ribs and my stomach ready to launch.

"Where are you?" I yelled suddenly, not certain whether it came from courage or terror. "I know you're in here!"

A breeze wafted through the opened door, warm yet chilling at the same time. My gaze darted to every shadow, every…

Oh-oh.

Behind the sectional.

I could see something dark, longish, and at first I wasn't quite sure what it was but my pipe jerked up a couple more inches.

Oh, goddammit!

An arm! It was a frickin' arm! I froze again, wondering if I could make it out through the slider door before that arm reached out and grabbed my ankle. I doubted it. The sectional was in the way and whoever that arm belonged to…

But that arm wasn't moving, was it? And if you were a psycho hellkiller would you leave your arm sticking out so your victim could spot it?

I wasn't sure. I didn't really know how psycho hellkillers thought. I didn't want to know how psycho hellkillers thought. No good could come from that.

In motion again, against my better judgment I eased towards the couch. I couldn't even feel my fingers now, they were clamped so tightly to the pipe.

A thought leaped into my mind: Whoever that arm belonged to was dead. Dead-dead-dead.

No kidding, a voice screamed in my mind. Harlen had been dead a year.

No, I thought, not Harlen.

I came around the couch and that scream I was telling you about? Yup, full force and nearly strong enough to tear the lining right out of my throat. I don't even know how long I was shrieking because even after I stopped it was still ringing in my ears.

That arm belonged to someone dead all right, someone in a blue uniform to whom it was no longer attached. Four feet away from the arm, behind the sectional, lay the body of a cop, and even in the semi-darkness I could see his chest and throat had been ripped open. Organs and pieces of the body were strewn all about like gory garland, and an ocean of blood had spread across my cream-colored carpet. An odor assailed my nostrils, and bile surged into my throat. It was the stench of an abattoir, sickly warm and coppery, yet worse, indescribable. The head had been nearly severed from the body and the officer's terror-glazed eyes stared at me as if damning me for ever being put on the assignment to protect a worthless stripper from something no human could ever combat.

I shrieked again. I couldn't help it. I wanted to be brave and controlled like all those investigators in crime scene movies but I didn't have it in me. Nobody was supposed to witness something like this, no one was supposed to see such a depraved violation of a human body.

I spun, my only thought now to run before my terror completely overwhelmed me and I passed out.

"Miss me?" Harlen said and I damn near collapsed.

THIRTY-SIX

The Old Slice and Dice

I don't know what kept me conscious other than some deep-seated instinct for survival. I had spun right into Harlen, who stood there grinning a ghoulish grin, half his face mangled and the evidence of Pete's shotgun blasts showing plainly on his ragged torso. He must have been hiding behind the counter in the kitchen, waiting for me to discover the murdered cop. In his hand, moonlight glinting from its razor-edged blade, he held a knife caked with gore.

My scream stopped. His arm came up, poised to plunge the knife into my chest. This time I didn't freeze. My survival instinct kicking in, I jerked up the pipe and slammed it into the intact side of his face. A sickening crunch sounded as the pipe hit, caving bone.

Harlen stumbled back a step, his knife had coming down, missing me by about the width of my G-string. Then he started laughing. Definitely not the reaction I was hoping for.

"Nice try, bitch," he said, voice grating, hollow.

I was deadmeat. I've said that before and gotten lucky but this time my luck had run out, because I had hit the sucker full force with a metal pipe and he was still standing there, grinning at me, all grosslike.

He stepped forward, jerking up the knife. I let him have it with the pipe a second time, catching him clean against the side of the skull. Another satisfying yet worthless crunch sounded. I think I saw brain matter but didn't get time to dwell on it.

Harlen let out a yell this time. Well, it was more like a roar. Even in the semi-darkness I saw death in his eyes—my death.

Then the world went black and white. Everything around me totally crapped color and the chiming strains of *Calcutta* rang out. It might have startled me but it stopped Harlen dead, so to speak.

I saw him in the corner, then, Lamont, his arm raised across his lower face, a shuddery laugh echoing above the music.

Who knows what crimes cripple the minds of the guilty...

Oh, swell, just swell. A ghost dressed as a mythical TV character was coming to my rescue. Not that I am one to look a gift ghost in the mouth, but, I mean, really...

Harlen must have thought the same thing because the manifestation stopped him only an instant. He lunged, knife poised for the kill.

I might have had only a couple of weeks of karate training but I knew enough to get the hell out of the way when charged by a psycho hellkiller, at least this time.

The knife slashed above my head, nearly taking off my bun, and I fell against the couch, banging a shin on the coffee table in the process. I let out a word unsuitable for church and rebounded, not sure what force of will was driving me, and tried to slam him again with the pipe. I missed his head but the tip caught his knife hand and by shear dumb luck the blade went flying.

Around me, the Lamont's laughter and the music kept rising, but it wasn't doing a damn bit of good. It only made everything more terrifyingly surreal. I wasn't ready to die in black and white. I wasn't ready to die in color, for that matter.

Harlen's arm swept up, and I tried to duck but his fist glanced off my face and I flew backward over the couch. The pipe spiraled from my hand and landed on the carpet a half-dozen feet away.

I might have blacked out, then. I wanted to. I wanted to just go away to some other place where I could be blissfully unaware of the ripper chopping my corpse up into bite-size pieces. I think the only thing that prevented it was the fact that I landed right atop the mutilated cop's body. Blood once it's out of the body feels incredibly cold. It might be just the thought that it was once *inside* the body that makes it feel that way but whatever the case the murdered cop's blood soaked my T-shirt and smeared across my bare arms. The slick feel of exposed organs beneath my hands as I struggled to push myself off the corpse made me start to retch.

Making inarticulate sounds of terror, I scrambled off the cop, slipping on the blood-soaked carpet. I saw Harlen coming around the couch, looming like a great predator about to pounce on its tiny blonde prey. I screamed, and screamed. And screamed.

I don't think I stopped screaming even as the world flashed to glaring streamers of bright white and color.

THIRTY-SEVEN

In the Light of a Clear Blue Corpse

My own condo lights, I realized, my mind spinning and terror sweeping through me in a hellish cyclone.

Then thunder crashed out. From everywhere. Bursts of it.

"Stay down, Chloe!" I heard someone scream and it only barely penetrated my numbed mind it was Sturdevant.

More thunder. Shots. I saw Harlen stagger under their impact. I don't know how many bullets hit him, only that they had very little effect other than to knock him around. Pieces of his grayish flesh flew off and maybe an ear and a finger ended up on the carpet.

Cops poured through the slider and in from the front door, which I think somebody had kicked in. It happened in an unreal blur and I'm not even entirely sure of all the details.

I *was* sure Harlen wasn't going down unless the bullets chopped him into little pieces and maybe even the pieces would still be moving, like in that old movie with the crawling severed hand. I think the cops realized it, too, because the shooting stopped and they rushed him.

That was a mistake, but who can blame them for misjudging? Harlen was unlike anything the pragmatic boys in blue had ever faced. He was no bank robber or wife beater. He was a corpse. A living corpse.

And he responded appropriately. He flung them aside as if they were annoying puppies biting at his ankles. One tumbled over the sectional and another bounded over the coffee table. A third was hurled backward, feet coming completely off the floor; he ricocheted off a wall, leaving a caved-in oval roughly three feet in diameter.

I grabbed the back of the couch, tried to pull myself up. Three cops were struggling to pin Harlen's arms, get them twisted behind his back and into cuffs, but were losing the battle. Harlen himself was an ani-mated mass of grayish craters where bullets had impacted, and not a lot remained of his features. Pieces of flesh hung off his torn-up chest and arms and bones poked through his cheeks and ribs.

Johnny was on the floor, where Harlen had thrown him, shaking his head. It occurred to me it was a good thing Harlen didn't still have his knife because there would have been more dead cops lying about my apartment.

I struggled to my feet, knowing they weren't going to be able to stop him. "Christ, Bob, this better work..." I muttered, partially in shock, but something in my mind driving me to do the only thing I could think of doing before everybody ended up dead. I grabbed the chain from around my neck and flung myself at Harlen. I got the ring over his staved-in head, choking back revulsion and the bile that surged into my throat.

Roaring again, Harlen hurled the three cops off him. I went back-ward, landing against the couch arm and toppling over.

Harlen hesitated, his hand going to the ring dangling about his neck. I waited for him to dissolve, the way Praetallious had, but he let out an unearthly laugh.

"I've been looking for that..." he said, voice eerily hollow.

Oh, crap. The ring had no effect on him whatsoever. What was the old adage about never trying the same trick twice?

Sturdevant got shakily to his feet again and fired a shot as Harlen took a step towards me. The killer jerked and another small piece of him landed on my carpet.

Sturdevant blasted the ripper again and again, emptying his gun, and even then kept pulling the trigger, as if he were in shock. Harlen jerked with each shot, but did not go down. He wavered, as if he might fall, but a moment later just staggered towards the slider doors, knock-ing aside cops who tried to stop him.

More shots came as Harlen stumbled out into the night. I am pretty sure most of them hit, but it made no difference. They had succeeded in chasing him off for the moment but they hadn't killed him. They couldn't kill him.

I am not sure what happened next because I ran to the kitchen, grabbed the trashcan and heaved. Then I sat on the floor and passed out.

THIRTY-EIGHT

Hell's Aftermath

"**Y**ou ok?" John Sturdevant asked as we stood in my kitchen, him giving me an I-told-you-you-should-have-called-Arlo look along with the one of concern.

I nodded, my hands clamped around a cup of jasmine tea. I took a sip, trying to get the lingering taste of vomit in my mouth to go away. After he'd revived me, I'd gone upstairs and changed from my blood-stained T-shirt into a yellow sweater and jeans. I'd spent an hour in the bathroom, cleaning up, trying to scrub all the blood off my body. I felt like I'd never be able to wash it all off, like it had somehow seeped into my pores and my very soul. The acrid gunmetal odor of it still assailed my nostrils. The worst part was I knew I was never going to get the ghastly sight of that murdered policeman out of my nightmares. Every time I closed my eyes his terror-stricken gaze would haunt me.

Cops still roamed my apartment, putting up yellow tape like it was Christmas garland and collecting the samples of grayish flesh Harlen had left on my carpet. Their faces were fraught with shock and questions as to just what the hell had happened here tonight. Johnny knew about things that went bump in the night but they did not. They were just ordinary workaday blues with no taste for killers who absorbed dozens of bullets and walked away.

"How are you going to explain it to them?" I asked Johnny, my voice steadier than I would have expected.

He shook his head and let out a grunt. "I wish to hell I knew. I can't. There is no explanation for something like that. Too many of us saw it. Too many saw a man take a barrage of gunfire and still walk away."

"How did you come to be here, Johnny?" I shuddered, knowing if he hadn't been I would be in the same condition as that mutilated cop.

"Samulson didn't check in at his normal time so I tried calling your number and got a busy signal. I tried your cell, too, and that went to voice mail."

"It was in my backpack down here. I never heard it ring."

He nodded. "I knew something was wrong and had a pretty good idea what it was. I brought ten men with me, Chloe. Ten men and we couldn't stop him. Three of those men are in the hospital now with broken arms and ribs and one man…"

I could feel the blood drain from my face. "I know. It was horrible."

"He had a wife and two kids. How the hell am I going to tell them an indestructible killer murdered him, cut him into pieces?"

I didn't have an answer for him and I knew he didn't expect one. "Lamont showed up right before you did."

He sighed, his own face as white as I had ever seen it. "So, is he associated with Harlen?"

I shook my head. "He was trying to save me. I'm positive this time. But there wasn't anything he could do. I don't think he has the power to do much more than manifest himself, along with pieces of his past. He wanted to show me more at the theater but couldn't and we were interrupted before he could tell me everything."

"How did Harlen react to him?"

"He hesitated. I know he was able to see Lamont where most ordinary people can't."

"Harlen's not exactly ordinary people anymore."

"Didn't matter to him, which just proves Lamont isn't here to harm me and not part of the escapees from Hell deal."

"You can't stay here, Chlo. And you have to call Arlo."

My gaze lifted to the slider, where in the distance I could see the sky brightening with the first light of dawn. I was exhausted but knew I couldn't have slept had I wanted to. "I'll stay at Arly's house and bring the cat, for all the protection he was worth."

"And Arlo?"

"I'll call him. I'll tell him everything."

"You don't, I will, Chlo."

I nodded, frowned. "I will, Johnny." I paused, the night's events racing through my mind. Nausea welled in my belly again. I took a sip of tea, but it didn't help. "The ring had no effect on him."

He gave me a grim expression. "That fact didn't escape me."

"It wasn't like with Praetallious. I thought the ring would kill Harlen but it didn't. He seemed glad to have it. Like it belonged to him or something."

"Then why did Lansing want you to have it?"

"That's a damn good question, isn't it?"

"I don't trust her."

With a shrug, I said, "I don't, either. But maybe I just assumed she had given me that thing for the same reason."

"Whatever the case I want to bring her in for questioning."

"For what? Illegal gift-giving by a monkey?"

He sighed, knowing I was right and there was nothing he could stick on her or bring to a judge to get a warrant for her arrest. And I had the notion that if she didn't want to be found, she wouldn't be anyway.

THIRTY-NINE

Pixie Sticks

Puddin' Head didn't look the least bit happy about being displaced, but I figured he would have been a whole lot more unhappy being left back at the townhouse with all those cops crawling around and nobody to feed him. I hauled his fuzzy butt out of the car after I parked in the driveway of Arly's cottage house and headed for the door. I had my backpack slung over my shoulder and the key Arly had given me out of my pocket and in hand.

The early morning sun was just hovering over the eastern horizon and everything looked strangely amber, like I had stepped into another world, but amber was a hell of a lot better than black and white. And red. Red wasn't my favorite color at the moment because I'd seen enough blood in my apartment to last me a lifetime. I still couldn't get the image of the dead cop out of my mind, nor the sight of Harlen, or what was left of Harlen, trying to kill me.

A surge of nausea threatened to make me lean over the porch rail and heave again but I managed to hold it down. I was glad of that because getting vomit out of cat fur wouldn't have thrilled either me or His Majesty very much.

After I shoved the door open, I set His Majesty on the floor and closed it behind me.

"You're going on a diet," I told him, half the feeling in my arm gone. I think he understood me because his tail shot up and he pranced off towards the living room.

I tossed my backpack on the table and leaned back against the door. Sunlight slanted through the window above the sink and I let out a sigh. I wanted to cry. I'd been trying to tell myself how strong I was but it wasn't washing. Because it didn't matter. What I had seen and been through during the night and over the past few months was more than any one person should have to experience in a lifetime. In four lifetimes. I'd nearly been killed by witches, a zombie, a plague-spreading demon and now a reanimated psycho hellkiller. And something told me even if I got through Harlen worse things were coming. I'd dreamt of Ficatier. She was coming back. I knew it in my soul and I wondered if there would ever be, could ever be, an end to all this that didn't involve Arly or myself, or everyone we cared about, getting killed. I'd lost everybody in my life I'd ever loved. I couldn't lose anyone else, even my ingrate cat, or I would just come apart.

Maybe that would be better, I thought. To just lose it, go crazy and be put away where Evil couldn't find me.

I laughed without humor. That wasn't exactly being realistic, was it? Because Evil would find me anywhere I went and being crazy would just make me more vulnerable.

You're special; Arlo's special, Lansing had said. Why? Why me? Why him? It didn't prevent us from being killed, at least in my case. Evil wanted Arly alive, but me, I guess I was expendable as long as they had him and that's why I had lied to Sturdevant. I was not going to call Arly this morning and tell him what happened. Not until I took care of Lamont and Harlen. With Lamont I now had an idea. A conduit. That's what I was to him and with a clarity that only came with having the crap shocked out of you, I had a theory how to proceed on that point. And after I got a couple hours sleep, assuming I could sleep, I would see about that.

Harlen was another story. I had no idea what to do about him since the ring hadn't worked the way I expected it to.

Exhaustion was making my head spin and I pushed myself away from the door, went to the counter and put on a fresh pot of coffee. I heard Puddin' Head let out a meow from the living room and wondered what his problem was now. Usually he'd settle in anywhere that included throw pillows or a really comfortable couch.

I went to the living room, spotted him sitting on a foot rest in front of the couch, looking at me like I had three heads. Amber light arced through the blinds, falling over the cedar chest beneath the window and glinting from the widescreen TV—the *new* widescreen TV I'd bought Arly a week ago, since I'd had a little mishap with the old one and a table lamp. Down the hall I heard the grandfather clock chime.

"At least one of us is capable of relaxing," I said to the cat, figuring I must have mistaken his meow of distress for one of contentment. Or maybe the cat was losing it.

A noise caught my attention, a thin clacking sound, and I whirled, my heart jumping into at my throat.

"Jesus!" I yipped, almost peeing myself again.

She stood behind me, near the fireplace whose mantle held a tri-frame of Arly and his two sons, Bobby and David. Dressed in a loose flower-print skirt that ended below her knees and an amorphous blue top was Ms. Genie Lansing, the New Salem Museum of Natural History's enigmatic director. Her white-blonde hair, pixyish in cut, curled into her small face and beneath her chin. The sound I had heard was that of her multi-colored plastic bracelets on each wrist clacking together.

"I didn't mean to startle you," she said and a little lilt came in her little prissy voice that said, oh yes the hell she did.

"You picked a frickin' poor time to go around scaring the crap out of me," I said, annoyed as hell and letting it bleed all over my voice. "I've had enough frights for one night."

She nodded, her misty marble eyes oddly amused. I wanted to bitch slap her. "So I heard."

"Oh, did you?" I wrapped my arms about myself to keep from going over and throttling her. "And just *how* would you have heard, Lansing? How do you hear anything?"

She smiled. A nasty little thing. "Like anyone else, police radio."

I had big doubts what had happened had gone out over the police radio in any detail other than the call that summoned them all to my apartment, but I had learned sparring with her was damn near useless.

"My ass," I said. "What are you doing here? And how did you get in? In fact, how do you manage to come and go like a ghost, anyway?" I had her cornered now and it was about damn time she answered some questions.

"The back door was unlocked."

She was lying. "Arly's a cop, he doesn't leave doors unlocked when he's out of town and I've checked the house a couple times."

Her little smile got patronizing. "You've been though a lot, you must have overlooked it."

Now, I wanted to slap her even harder. "What are you doing here?"

"I wanted to see you."

"That's kind of funny, because I've been tying to see you for two weeks and you've made yourself damn scarce."

"What you wanted from me I couldn't give you."

"Yeah? Let me guess, you're not allowed to interfere."

"That's right."

"And yet, here you are." I paused. "And how the hell would you know I was here anyway?"

"I went to your apartment first. Detective Sturdevant told me you were coming here."

Another lie, I was sure. Johnny wouldn't have told her; he would have driven her over. But she *was* here and that point was unarguable.

"I want to know about my sister."

"I've told you all I can."

"I don't' think so."

"All right, all I am allowed to tell, then."

"For a chick who keeps saying that, you and your little furry pal spend an awful lot of time getting into my business."

"You have something of mine. I'd like it back."

"Oh? Really? And what might that be?" I wanted to say "Arly?" but refrained. I think she might have gotten the implication anyway because the patronizing smile on Ms. Pixie Sticks' thin lips got a bit more acute.

"A ring."

"Come again?"

"You know the one I mean. Upraised symbols and a devil face, black stone."

"Oh, I know it damn well, but you gave it to me. Now you want it back?" Had Pixie Sticks flipped her white-blonde wig?

A frustrated glint appeared in her eyes for the first time. "I didn't give it to you. You weren't meant to have it."

"Well, your monkey must have missed the memo."

She frowned, the frustration bleeding onto her face now. "He wasn't supposed to give it to you."

"Then why did he?"

"He felt you should have it, as a warning. I did not."

My brow furrowed. Maybe I wasn't the crazy one after all. "Uh, we *are* talking about a monkey here, right?"

She nodded. "We have our disagreements…"

"You and the monkey? You have differences of opinions?"

She looked at me like she thought I should think that was normal. I talked to my cat more than I should, so maybe I couldn't be too judgmental.

"He thought it would warn you, I thought it might...confuse you." She said "confuse you" like she thought I was an idiot.

"And you couldn't have just called and told me this before the psycho hellkiller broke into my apartment? That ring almost got me killed tonight. Bob might as well have given me a target to put on my back."

"You're a target anyway. You will always be for what escaped. They know where to find you when they want you."

I let out a huge sigh, but she wasn't telling me anything I didn't already suspect. "Comforting as that is, why didn't that ring stop him, the way the locket did Praetallious?"

"It is not a protection charm of any sort. The ring belonged to a man named Tumblety, a man of certain gruesome persuasions in the 19th century."

"Gruesome persuasions?" I suddenly recalled the book opened to a page about Jack the Ripper and the Tumblety name had an odd familiarity to it. "What exactly is this ring?"

She moved away from the fireplace, glancing at my cat, then looking back to me. "It's symbolic, mostly. Tumblety wore that ring as he committed certain...crimes. The ring identified him to others of his ilk."

"Others meaning?"

"Those in the Cult of Phraitemporicus."

"Phraitemporicus?"

"Must you repeat everything I say?"

I smirked, glad I had irritated her. "Well, yeah, pretty much, because I don't know who the hell that is or what you're getting at."

She shook her head, giving me one of the put out looks I normally reserved for my cat.

"Phraitemporicus, a demon given to great cravings for lust and blood. The cult that formed around his worship focused on the sacrifice of women, generally women who were of a certain persuasion."

"What kind of persuasion?"

I didn't care a hell of a lot for her smile. "Prostitutes, wanton women...*strippers*..."

Ah, she was an inch away from me jamming a shoe down her throat. "Was Tumblety...Jack the Ripper?"

"If I told you that there wouldn't be much mystery left in the world, would there?"

Er, was that a joke from Ms. Stick Up the Ass? I think it might have been. "What does it have to do with Harlen? Was he a worshiper?"

She nodded. "That ring belonged to him. I took it from his body…while he was at the morgue."

"And you couldn't have warned me about that before he attacked me—twice?"

"I'm not allowed to—"

"Interfere, yeah-yeah, second verse same as the first. And now you want your ring back, why?"

"There are only five of those rings. That is the first one I have been able to locate."

I folded my arms. "That still doesn't answer my question. What about it is so important to you?"

Now it was her turn to look a little uncomfortable. She didn't want to tell me, but she knew if there was any chance of getting that ring back she was going to have to. Good thing she had no idea I didn't have it. Apparently she wasn't as all-knowing as I had started to think.

"I can't tell you," she said at last. That just pissed me off.

"You'd better, if you think you've got a chance in Hell, pardon the expression, of getting that ring back." I hoped she couldn't tell I was lying.

More frowning and her misty marble eyes narrowed. "There are objects in this world, Miss Everson. Objects that were forged with the blood of innocents and imbued with power, but only with a portion of it. Those objects, should all of them be put together, however, have the ability to do certain things. In this case, the rings can raise Phraitemporicus. This demon is not on Czcarabas' level, but if he returns he could cause a horrendous amount of destruction and death."

"And you say there are five of these rings?"

"Five. I have—had—one…until Bob gave it to you."

"Because he wanted to warn me?"

She nodded. "He's developed an affinity for you for some reason I can't imagine, but he's male so his standards aren't the highest."

Eeew, she had just about gotten on my last frickin' nerve with that remark. "And how do I know you just don't want all five for yourself, to bring back this demon?"

She laughed and it wasn't a particularly nice laugh. It was a laugh that said, *what an idiot*. Meaning yours truly. "I gave Arlo Grimm the sword to vanquish Ficatier, and I gave you the locket to dispose of Praetallious…"

I shrugged, trying to keep some dignity and look like I knew what I was talking about. "Maybe you did that to gain my confidence, and use me or Arly to bring back one of those demons, the way Ficatier wants to."

"That is utter foolishness."

Does anyone talk that way anymore? For her roughly 25 years she seemed suddenly much older and I couldn't put my finger on why. "Well, you're piss out of luck because Harlen has the ring."

That annoyed her. Greatly. "You gave it to him?"

"I didn't *give* it to him, per se. I thought it would work like the locket and put it around his neck." Wow, that sounded really retarded when I said it out loud. Her look said that was just about the extent of it, too.

"It doesn't work that way all the time."

Um, duh.

"You have to get it back," she added.

"Me?" My voice went up a notch.

"You gave it to him."

"I didn't *give* it to him, I told you. I tried to destroy him."

"Well, destroy him and get it back."

"You got any clear idea just how I am s'posed to do that? The guy took an arsenal of bullets last night and energizer bunnied himself right out my door."

"How did he die originally?" she asked, and I think it was a legitimate question, not an *are-you-an-idiot?* one.

"He hanged himself in his cell."

"Then you have to hang him."

"Hang him? Are you frickin' serious? Just how am I supposed to do that? He ate his supernatural Wheaties."

"You could burn him, also."

"Oh, that's much better. Maybe I'll just throw him a barbecue."

"I don't care how you do it, just as long as you do."

She was frickin' serious. I mean, really. Her face looked like a little stone pixie. No humor, sarcastic or otherwise.

"That freak almost killed me last night and he did murder someone sent to protect me. He tossed around ten cops like they were dolls. He's butchered a number of young women. I can't even get close enough to him to set him on fire or get a noose around his neck."

She appeared unsympathetic. "You lost the ring."

"Your little baboon gave it to me."

"He's not a baboon, he's a—"

"Monkey, I know the difference. Turn of phrase, Ms. Literal."

I ran a hand through my hair and sighed. I had no desire even to get close to that freak again but what if she was telling the truth? What if those rings all ended up together and some demon starting raising literal hell on earth?

Why wasn't anything ever easy?

I pinned her with my gaze. "I don't trust you, Lansing. You come and go like some sort of ghost, you talk in riddles and are just about the most unhelpful bitch I've ever run across. And I think you've got your eye on something that isn't yours, and I know damn well you know what I mean."

"Don't you mean who?"

I nodded. "We understand each other."

"I don't think we do, Miss Everson, not completely. But now isn't the time to go into it. Just get that ring back."

I seriously didn't know what to do. Even if I could get the thing back and somehow turn Harlen into a crispy critter or stretch his neck, could I trust her enough to give her the ring?

"I'm not promising to give the thing to you, even if I do get it back, Lansing. Like I said, I don't trust you and unless you want to be a hell of a lot more forthcoming about who you are and what you're up to…"

She smiled, a smile that told me I shouldn't hold my breath. She went to the mantle, ran her fingertips along the tri-frame of Arlo and his sons, her bracelets clacking. "You should talk to David, Miss Everson. About your dream…"

Surprise made my stomach dip. "How did you know about that?"

No expression on her face this time. "You'd be surprised what I know about dreams, visions. Ficatier's still a problem. She wouldn't have been had David not made a mistake. He thought by doing what he did…well, ask him about it."

"David's not exactly sociable."

Her brow lifted, fell. "No, I suppose he isn't."

Puddin' Head let out a meow and I glanced at him. He was peering in Lansing's direction and I looked back to her, about to ask her just how she had gotten here since I hadn't noticed any cars parked in the street or driveway when I drove in but she was no longer there. She had vanished, practically in front of my eyes, and I think somehow the cat had sensed it was going to happen.

I let out a long sigh. Monkeys and cats, who needed them?

FORTY

Date with a Ghost

"Hang him," she says. "Set him on fire," she says. "I argue with my monkey," she says. "Strippers are wanton women," she says. Well, ok, she didn't say that last one in so many words but the implication was pretty obvious. Whatever the case, Genie Lansing had gotten under my skin, not only for her lack of helpfulness for just about every other thing I could think of, most specifically her crushin' on my man. Pixie Sticks just irritated the hell out of me and there was no other way around it.

I'd gotten about six hours worth of sleep after she left. I thought I wouldn't be able to sleep after what had happened in my apartment last night but after making sure Arly's doors were all locked—the back one was, incidentally, just as I thought, so little Ms. Priss couldn't have gotten in that way—I'd collapsed on the couch and before I knew it was out like the proverbial light. When I woke up, it took me another half hour and two cups of coffee to get rid of the grogginess and steady myself enough to drive.

Oh, and I peed before I left, because I had the feeling those two cups would be ready for launch by the time I reached the nursing home.

I pulled into the parking lot at Willow Pines, a strange sadness and depression swarming over me. I had the notion I knew what Lamont wanted me for, though I still had questions as to his timing. He needed me, or at least my sensitive ability, as a conduit, because Lillian Marlene apparently did not have that gift. Without it, he could not manifest himself to her directly. But did she have another gift, one that precipitated Lamont's emergence from ghostly mothballs after so many years? And how did that relate to Amanda's having been drawn to New Salem?

I wasn't totally sure, but I know Lamont wanted me here now and the dark feeling that went through me confirmed it. I wondered why he hadn't appeared yesterday when I'd visited Marlene with Amanda. Maybe he couldn't with her there for some reason known only to the supernatural boos throwing the dice.

Or I could be totally wrong and wasting my time coming here when I should have been searching for Harlen, though God knew how I was going to hang him or set him on fire and get that ring back before he cut me into little pieces.

Don't worry, another voice inside me said, Harlen knows where to find you when he wants you. He's just off licking his wounds. Oh, yeah, that was just a real comfort. Crap on a cracker, I couldn't deal with that right now. Harlen could find me, I felt sure, and would, but at the moment I had another mission and I am pretty sure it involved a ghostly reunion.

I got out of the car, stared at the brick exterior of the place. I waited for the world to turn black and white, but it didn't. I started to doubt my piece of detective work. Ok, so it wasn't so much detective work as stripper's—you know, those wanton women Lansing mentioned?—intuition, but Lamont's manifestations centered around his old role at the theater and Lillian Marlene, and Lillian Marlene, from the looks of her, didn't have a whole lot of time left. If Lamont needed me to contact her he damn well better get his ass in gear.

"If you want something from me, you better do it now, bub," I muttered, trying to sound more brave than I actually felt. It was still a ghost I was dealing with, after all, and though he wasn't threatening I was still experiencing that locked-in-a-dark-cellar feeling I had as a child.

I started towards the building, my mind racing. Brant Lamont and Lillian Marlene. Amanda Conners. Genie Lansing. Carlis Harlen. Me and Arly. Witches and reanimated demons. I saw separate fates, but also fates that intertwined. And a future where the stakes got higher and the attacks from the other side got stronger and more frequent.

Until Angelique Ficatier returned.

I shivered, chewed on my lower lip. Damn, scared myself. I was doing a lot of that lately, but I think I had good reason to.

FORTY-ONE

A Room with No View

The depressive feeling increased the moment I stepped into the building and any uncertainty faded. The dinner hour quickly approaching, so the stench of canned greenbeans and a host of unidentifiable odors assailed my nostrils, making me queasy. Walking down the long gloomy hallway, I noticed nobody manned the front desk and wondered if Marlene would even be in the meeting room at four in the afternoon. If she wasn't, I'd have to locate a desk nurse and get a room number.

As I stepped into the room a blast of heat hit me. The fireplace blazed away and the air felt heavy, moist.

I let out a small sigh of relief upon seeing Marlene sitting near the window, in nearly the same spot Amanda and I had left her yesterday. Again I was struck by an utter sense of loneliness, of life gone by. I hoped I never had to visit one of these places after today and again I prayed I was never in one, though Evil didn't appear inclined to let me reach an age at which that would be necessary.

I started across the room, which was unoccupied except for Marlene, getting more depressed by the second, the feeling both external and internal.

Lamont. It had to be. He was close, waiting for the right moment, though I wasn't exactly sure what that moment was. I didn't think I'd have to wait long to find out.

Stopping behind Marlene's wheelchair, not sure exactly what was s'posed to happen, only expecting that something would, I stared at her white hair and frail shoulders.

"Miss Connors?" I said, knowing full well she couldn't answer but wanting to let her know I was there. "Miss Connors, I know this is going to sound crazy, but…somebody sent me to see you. I think that somebody wants…*needs* to reach you, tell you something important."

I waited but nothing happened. No fade to noir, no whispery laugh. Nada. Had I been wrong, after all?

Wait a minute. Her shoulders. Her shoulders showed no motion, not the slightest up and down movement expected of a living, breathing person. Something plunged in my belly.

"Miss Connors?" I said again. "Please don't be…"

Dead.

That word again. I started to feel light-headed with dread. "Oh, God…" I whispered as I gripped the handles and swung her chair around. Her head slumped forward, chin landing on her chest. Her milky eyes were open, staring blankly, unseeing. A string of drool snaked from the corner of her bluish lips.

Oh, crap on a cracker.

I knew before I even touched her thin wrist to check for a pulse Lillian Marlene had played her final role in life.

But before I could think about it further, the world turned to black and white.

FORTY-TWO

A Sliver of Darkness

The change told me part of my answer. Lamont hadn't appeared yesterday when I was here with Amanda because he knew, somehow, Marlene didn't have just very little time left, she had *none*. He needed me here the moment of her death or at least close to her passing, which made me certain my decision to come here hadn't entirely been my stripper's intuition, but an otherworldly whisper.

Calcutta began playing low somewhere, like it was filtering out of the old radio on the stage at the theater—

"You can't leave!" a voice screamed from behind me and I whirled. The nursing home room melted away. Tables, chairs, everything just dripped out of the scene, suddenly replaced by a stage and rows of velvet-padded seats. I now stood in the New Salem Theater again. Lillian Marlene, a young Lillian Marlene, knelt beside the pile of bricks and Lamont was walking away from her, picking up where the scene had left off yesterday.

"Lillian…" he said, voice exasperated, yet also holding resolve and a hint of sadness. He glanced back at her, stopping a moment. "It has to be this way and you know it. Neither of us will have a career if you go through with it."

"I have to, Brant!" she yelled, tears streaming from her eyes, her pleading face turned up to him. She wasn't acting; there was no faking that kind of emotional pain. "It's part of us."

He made a sound that said he didn't give a damn, but his eyes said different. "It is a mistake and you need to fix it. The studio will fix it." With that he turned and started walking away again.

"Don't you walk away from me!" she shrieked, tears streaming harder. "Don't you walk away from *us!*"

"I already have, Lillian," he said, voice low. "I did the moment I met you."

"Nooo!" Her screech could have peeled paint off a wall. I don't think I have ever heard anything quite so agonized and I was certain now she loved him, and that something further was compelling her to try to cling to an arrogant man concerned solely with rebuilding his career. I'm not sure if her mind snapped then, four years before her breakdown, or it this was merely the event that precipitated it. Whatever the case, Lillian Marlene's grip on her own sanity faltered.

She grabbed one of the bricks from a pile beside her and came to her feet in one ungraceful movement. She stumbled forward and Lamont turned at the sound of her clumsy footfalls.

But didn't turn soon enough.

She brought the brick down on his skull and blood splattered across his face and her hand. He staggered, eyes wide, stunned, flashing disbelief and the reflection of his own death. She screamed, any control over her own actions now impossible in a raging sea of blind hurt. She brought the brick down again, again, again.

Lamont collapsed, all life draining from his eyes. His body hit the floor hard, didn't move.

My hands went to my mouth, and I suppressed a gasp of shock and revulsion. Yet I could not stop watching as she stared at what she had done, tears streaming onto Lamont's unmoving form. She crumpled to her knees, throwing herself over his body and sobbing for long moments.

As the song ended, leaving cold silence, she came up, icy indifference now in her eyes, a dark instinct for survival accompanying it. She got to her feet, grabbed him under the arms and struggled to drag him backward to the partially completed wall beside the stage. It took her some effort to get his body up over a three-foot finished section and dump him into the compartment behind it.

Then she looked at me and I knew for the first time she actually saw me. Behind her the wall was suddenly finished, bricked up.

"I called a workman I knew had a thing for me," she said, her voice soft, emotionless. "I screwed him after to make sure he'd keep his mouth shut about finishing the wall, but I don't think he ever saw the body."

"You killed him..." I said, stating the obvious, unsure what else to say.

"She did," another voice came from beside me and I nearly jumped out of my jeans. Lamont, sitting in a theater seat, gazed up at me, then at her. Marlene looked at him, still no emotion on her face.

"You needed me as a conduit," I said, not really a question.

He nodded and stood. "But she needed to die first. And I needed to be stronger."

"Did you draw Amanda here?"

A puzzled look crossed his face, which was now completely visible. He still wore the cape but the hat was on the stage.

"No...no, I believe that was Lillian who summoned her. That's *her* gift."

"What about Harlen?" I asked.

He frowned. "He's...something else. I tried to warn you."

"I know you did. I appreciate it but you could have just said, hey there's a psycho hellkiller after you."

"No, I was not—"

I held up my hand. "I know, allowed. Old story."

He gave me a grim smile. "There are rules, Chloe."

"Which seem to get broken on a whim."

"Then there are consequences."

I wondered if Lansing had been dealt any consequences for her help with Ficatier and Praetallious; it sure didn't look that way.

"I did love you, Lillian," he said, stepping past me and going to the woman. He placed his hands on her shoulders.

"I know..." she whispered, a tear slipping down her cheek.

"I was foolish, couldn't see past my own selfishness." He kissed her forehead and it might have been a warm moment had they both not been frickin' dead.

"I was enraged..." Emotion finally bled into Marlene's voice, and her lower lip quivered. "I couldn't face life without you, knowing there would be other women...I called you back, Brant. I had to tell you I was sorry before I went...I never meant..."

He nodded, took her in his arms. "I know you didn't."

"I called *her* back, too. I did it years ago, but she didn't come...I don't know why."

"She couldn't. Her path…" He looked back to me and I wondered what the hell they were talking about. "She needed Chloe to be here in New Salem, needed the time to be right. It wasn't right, then."

Huh? The more I learned the more confused I got. Marlene had murdered Lamont and stuffed him behind a wall—oh, cripes, Johnny was going to love it when I told him he had to knock down a wall at the theater, so was his little date—because he rejected her love? Why did I suddenly feel like I was stuck in a cheesy romance novel? Except for the dead people part, of course.

Then, after sexually bribing someone to brick it up and keep quiet, Marlene had gone on with her life and had a breakdown because she couldn't handle the guilt?

No, there was something more, wasn't there? And it was starting to penetrate my thick head just what that something was, *who* it was.

"I saw our baby, Brant. She's beautiful…" Marlene said, still holding him. They were fading, becoming almost transparent.

"I know. I knew she would be."

"If she had gotten the chance…" Marlene said, her voice soft and distant, now.

Lamont looked back to me and a silent thank you came from his lips. Around me color was seeping into the world, slowly this time, and theater seats and stage were vanishing.

A moment later I was back in the nursing home meeting room and fading sunlight had turned the place gloomy, but the depressive sensation was gone.

Marlene and Lamont were gone, too, and I knew I wouldn't see either of them again. He had come back to forgive her after her love and guilt had summoned him from decades of dead. And lucky me, I was just the wireless service.

I glanced at the old woman's body in the chair. Her baby, she had said.

The rest of the puzzle.

Crap on a cracker.

FORTY-THREE

Lives Never Lived

As dusk turned the world to shimmering shades of gray-blue, I pulled up in front of Lillian Marlene's cottage. I sat behind the wheel, staring at the decrepit place, knowing now what I had seen in a young woman's eyes besides sadness. Loss. Regret for a life never lived. I wanted to cry. My throat tightened and my belly fluttered with emotion.

At this point I didn't really know if I could feel sorry for Marlene and Lamont's twisted little love story, because, after all, he had been an arrogant philandering sonofabitch and she a gold-digging murderess, but if they could forgive each other, who was I not to forgive them, too? I would have to think about it.

But I did feel sorry for one person, and it was turning my heart inside-out.

My phone chimed and I started, then fished it out of my backpack and flipped it open.

"Chlo?"

"Who else would be answering my phone, Johnny?" I tried to make it humorous but I wasn't in the mood so it probably sounded bitchy.

He ignored it; he knew I'd been through hell the past few days.

"I came across something strange when I was searching through death notifications for Marlene…"

I nodded, though he couldn't see me. "I know what it is."

"Dammit, Chloe, just for once I wish you'd let me have my moment."

I uttered a small laugh. "You can have some of mine. I'm getting way too many."

"I don't want yours. Yours come with zombies."

"How old?" I asked.

"Three years, a handful of months."

"Thanks, Johnny." I flipped the phone shut and stuffed it into my backpack.

I got out of the car like I was going to a funeral. I guess in a way I was. I knew now what unfinished business Lamont had referred to—the reason for their break up, the catalyst that brought about Marlene's love and his murder, as well as her breakdown.

I went to the door, didn't bother to knock. I turned the handle; unlocked. I figured it would be. She was waiting for me, now, wasn't she?

I entered the house, finding myself in a small parlor. Gloomy was the best word I had to describe it. Gloomy and foreboding, with furniture covered with yellowed sheets, cobwebs streaming from a fireplace mantle, from the ceiling, and cloistered in shadowy corners. A thick coating of dust blanketed the hardwood floor and an oval carpet that lay before the couch.

She stood by a window, peering out, her arms wrapped about herself.

"When did you figure it out?" Amanda Connors-Marlene asked me without turning.

I came deeper into the room. "Probably the moment your mother said she had seen her baby. But I knew there was something else, something more than just the both of them forgiving each other. Lamont said he didn't bring you back. Your mother did. It was her gift to summon the restless dead. She said she tried to do it before. If I take it right, that was when I first met you."

Amanda turned to me, the sadness in her eyes deeper than at any point in the past. "The time wasn't right. You needed to be in New Salem or I couldn't stay in this world, so I...went away."

"Why? Couldn't you just come here on your own?"

She hesitated, confusion briefly crossing her face. "I could have, but it would have done no good. I came back different than my father, stronger, though I never realized it. I could manifest myself to anyone as long as you were in the same town. They chose you as my conduit, just as they chose you for my father."

"They? Who are *they*, Amanda?"

A wan smile filtered across her lips, then vanished. "I can't tell you that, Chloe."

A sigh trickled from my soul. "Let me guess, you're not allowed."

"It amounts to that. But you'll meet them soon enough. They'll explain more about your...gift."

Gift wasn't exactly the word I would have used. "When did *you* figure it out, Amanda? Did you know when you came here she wasn't your great aunt, that she was your mother?"

She shook her head, leaned back against the wall. "No...no, I thought...I don't know, honestly. I never thought about my past or anyone in it. I only knew that I was drawn here to see my 'aunt' by something dark...that darkness was the grave, Chloe. Then, the other night, when you asked me about my parents...I started thinking about my past and realized I couldn't remember my mother or father. In fact, I couldn't remember anything about my childhood and growing up, or even becoming a dancer. I couldn't remember a single good time, bad time. Nothing about my life."

I nodded, a tear slipping from my eye. I had told myself I wasn't going to cry, but like so many other things I told myself it got lost in the moment. "Because you never had a life, Amanda."

"I know...I was three...sick..."

And she had died. A child. And it had resulted in her mother's emotional breakdown, ended her career.

"She loved you, Amanda. No matter what she was or what happened between her and Lamont. She refused to give you up and tried to go on without him, raise you, at least from what I can put together."

A thin smile framed her lips. "And a mother's love never dies, Chloe, even when the child does..."

"She's...gone, Amanda."

She nodded, lips quivering, tears flowing harder and I felt like coming apart inside. I never was any good with sad endings and it took all I had to keep myself together.

"I know...I have to go, now, too." She started to fade. "Thanks, Chloe. If I had gotten the chance to have a friend...I couldn't have asked for better one."

That did it. I burst into tears. Then she was gone and I stood alone in the darkening room, an incredible feeling of loneliness washing over me. *Now* I wanted to call Arly, *needed* to call him, and I wanted to find Pat and do a hundred other things I had always told myself I was going to do before it was too late, before my life was gone. Because some people never got that chance, never lived long enough to *really* live.

I settled for going home to my cat.

FORTY-FOUR

Puddin' Head Strikes Back

Life wasn't fair sometimes. I don't think I need to tell anyone that. The evil in this world get second chances to come back and cause whatever crap they want to cause and women like Amanda Connors don't even get the opportunity to live a complete life filled with whatever fate decides to bring them. Parents die and a sister gets taken away for some, while others blissfully go about stepping all over people without consequence or recrimination.

You can probably tell I wasn't in the best of moods by the time I got to Arly's house. Out of the three, I felt the worst for Amanda. She hadn't asked to be born out of whatever union Lamont and Marlene had consummated and she'd never gotten the chance to grow up and have her own hopes and dreams realized...or crushed.

Who knows, maybe things wouldn't have turned out well for her, coming from that situation, having an unstable mother who'd murdered her father. At least she should have gotten a shot at it. But she hadn't, and that was that.

I pulled into the driveway and shut off the engine, wishing I could shake my blues, but it wasn't entirely their fault. I still had Harlen to deal with somehow and what I had been through over the past few days had affected me more than I wanted to admit. I was going to call Arly when I got in and tell him everything. He wasn't going to be happy with me, but he knew I had an independent streak and believe me he could be stubborn as hell, too, so he'd understand. Eventually.

I went to the door and unlocked it, dusk shading into evening, shadowy grays deepening to blue-black. I wished I had remembered to leave a light on.

After closing the door, I tossed my backpack on the table, then went to the coffee pot and poured a cup of cold Hills Bros. It was better than nothing. I gulped it down and figured I would go out a little later and grab a pizza because Arly had no food in the place. I'd discovered that earlier this morning when I was hoping for at least a bagel. Arly's diet consisted mostly of cold pizza and those grease burgers Pete made for him at the Lagoon, anyway. That was going to change when I moved in, whether he liked it or not. And speaking of not liking things, I remembered I had forgotten His Majesty's Friskies, so that wasn't going to go over well, but I s'posed a pissed off cat was better than a psycho hellkiller. But just barely.

I went to the living room, stopped in the entrance to see Puddin' Head still on the footrest, though he was up on all fours instead of snoring and that certainly was not like him. I could barely make him out in the dusky darkness, but I could tell his fur was raised along his back and he was making some sort of odd hissy-fit sound I had never heard come out of him before.

A slithery feeling went down my spine and every thing inside seemed to freeze. That stripper sense I told you about? Went off like a monkey in a tiger cage.

Something was wrong. Bad wrong and I knew it, but I didn't know which way to move. The cat was eyeing something and it wasn't me, and suddenly the room was too damn dark for my comfort level.

My hand drifted out, feeling for the wall switch to my right. I flicked it on, and the two table lamps blazed.

The cat let out another hiss that jerked me from the spell that froze me where I stood. I spun in the direction in which the cat was looking and let out one of those mouse-across-the-feet-bleats.

"The cat doesn't like me much, Chloe..." Harlen said, standing in the shadows to the left of the window. His voice came out an unearthly grating thing and everything inside me screamed to run. But I couldn't and I knew it. He was only a few paces from me and by the time I tried to bolt he would be on me. He was too strong, too fast, and I didn't have a pipe this time.

"He doesn't like anyone," I said, voice trembling though I was trying to cover my terror with nervous humor. "Don't take it personally." Who would have thought corpses had self-esteem issues, anyway?

He made a sound that might have been a laugh, or maybe just some kind of corpse gas. It was hard to tell. Walking a little raggedly, his body a landscape of gray-black holes and flaps of grayish flesh hanging free, he took a couple steps towards me and I got a better look at the damage Sturdevant's men had inflicted on him last night. The bullets had done a pretty good job. Bones jutted out in weird angles from his collar and ribs, from his neck and shoulders. Something that might have once been his intestine dangled from his stomach like a gray-black snake. His head and face were still a staved-in mess and the ring still dangled about his neck. He had a new knife—the police had found the other one in my apartment—and lamplight glinted from the blade. I was pretty damn sure this one was a hell of a lot bigger, but maybe it just looked that way because I was scared out of my frickin' wits.

I wasn't going to get to call Arly, was I? Arly was going to come home from his vacation to find whatever was left of me scattered about his living room.

"You can't kill me," I said stupidly, edging into the room to the opposite end of the couch, getting it between me and the grotesque animated remains of Carlis Harlen. "I'm special; she might need me."

He laughed, a deep-throated thing full of mockery. "*She* isn't here and what can they do to me that hasn't already been done, Chloe? Look at me!" His voice climbed, rage filling it. "You think there's any place for me in their plans?"

"There won't be if you do this..." I was stalling, my mind racing, trying to think of a way to stop him somehow. Arly didn't exactly keep nooses lying around the place and I didn't smoke, so I didn't happen to have matches or a lighter on me.

"I saw you, Chloe. That time at the Lagoon. I wanted you that night. I wanted you more than I ever wanted any woman. I watched you dance, knew if only I could get you alone I could make you do things you'd never dreamt of doing. And then..." He took another two steps towards me, his gait awkward, and I knew I had made a mistake. I might have actually been able to make it through the kitchen and out the door. The bullets hadn't killed him but had done enough damage to slow him down. "And then I would have cut you in to pieces for my demon-god. It's what all you whores deserve."

"You psycho hellkiller types seriously need a new line. All women are whores, blah, blah, blah..." I was starting to babble. I had gotten around the couch now, between it and the footstool on which Puddin' Head still hissed. I kicked the stool, trying to get him to run, but apparently something about Harlen caused him to get territorial, as if he thought he were some sort of lion instead of a house cat. The idiot.

Harlen laughed again and I really hated the sound of it. Evil laughs a lot. Like everything is one big joke to them.

"You're one of them, Chloe, one of those whores. You were the only thing I could think about while I was in Hell. Every minute of every eternal night I thought about getting you alone…"

"You don't look in any condition to be even thinking about that, Harlen. There isn't enough Viagra in the Hell." My legs had turned to Jell-O and my heart pounded hard enough to punch through my chest. My gaze darted back and forth but I saw no way out of the room. He was between me and the exit, and the window was closed and locked. I didn't think I had enough strength to go through it and the glass would have sliced me pretty nearly as bad as Harlen intended to. And I'd be in no condition to run once I hit the lawn. He'd have me, then. He had me now.

"Get out!" I yelled at the cat, and gave the stool another kick. Harlen hurtled the couch, then, a lot more agile than I expected from the way he walked. He was missing some frickin' pieces but still solid as hell, pardon the expression.

I screamed, tried to dart to my left, but his free hand clamped about my arm and dead fingers gouged deep into my flesh. Pain radiated all the way to my fingertips and he hauled me back, then flung me to the right. I missed the foot stool, luckily for the cat, and landed flat on my back near an overstuffed chair.

Christ, that hurt, the thought flashed through my head, but it was nothing compared to what I was going to feel when his blade plunged into me.

"Don't run, Chloe, I'll make it nice and slow so you can enjoy it." He came towards me again, what was left of his face hideous in the lamplight.

Through sheer strength of will I pushed myself over onto my side, palms flat on the floor, legs shoving against the couch, trying to get it in front of him. The couch moved, barely, and did nothing to stop him.

I got to my feet, everything paining, dizzy, blackness starting to form at the corners of my mind and my legs threatening to give out and send me right back down again.

No, I wouldn't let myself black out. That would make it too easy for him and I wasn't going down that way. He grabbed my wrist hauled me around. The odor of rot filled my nostrils, sent bile surging into my throat. My entire body shook and I struggled, kicking at the Harlen's shins, hoping that somehow his legs would crumble and he'd collapse. No such luck.

"Nooo!" I screamed and Puddin' Head let out a shriek of his own, a cat shriek. It wasn't pretty. I tried to pull my wrist free but Harlen just held it, waiting. His fingers felt like cold snakeskin. He was enjoying this, enjoying my terror. He got off on it and this time I had no magic charm or Bob the monkey to save my ass.

I was going to die. And the worst thing about it was I knew Arly was going to find me, the same way he had found his wife years ago, murdered, slashed to ribbons. In my last moments all I could do was worry about him, not myself. He wouldn't survive another loved one being murdered. I knew him, I knew what losing his wife that way had done to him and losing me would be the end of it.

Whatever deep buried courage I possessed, that thought galvanized it. I started kicking frantically at Harlen, over and over, and thumping him with my free fist. Pieces of his flesh came lose, but my efforts had no noticeable effect on him whatsoever. He just held me there as I struggled, like a lion holding a kitten. I yanked backwards, jammed my knee into his groin, raked my heel down his shin. I jammed my fingers into his eyes, his throat, but he didn't budge.

He grew suddenly tired of the game and his knife arm jerked up, the blade glinting in the lamp light.

This was it. The blade would come down and in the next few minutes I lived while he sliced me up I would feel pain unlike any I had ever felt before. And Arly would find me. Butchered. Like his wife.

"You sonofabitch I won't let him see me that way!" I screamed.

I am not sure whether the sudden scream made him hesitate for a fraction or if it was my final yank to my left using all my weight, but the knife missed when it came down, slashing a huge slice from my sweater but doing little other damage. I had the stupid thought, *Dammit, that was a new sweater*, but instinct took over and I seized the slight reprieve, threw myself sideways, his hand still clamped to my wrist. He nearly lost his balance, one leg almost buckling. I tried to go with the momentum, pull him over completely off his feet, but he was too strong.

Still slightly off kilter, he jerked me towards him again and brought up knife up for a final plunge. My mouth came open in a shriek as the blade started its downward sweep.

By all rights I should have died right then. One thing saved me—that stupid cat I was always bitching about. Because when I shrieked Puddin' Head lost whatever weird nerve he'd developed and darted off the footstool, yowling at the top of his cat lungs. He leaped to the floor directly between Harlen's legs. Harlen's off balance tilt got a lot worse and where shots had taken pieces off it his right leg buckled slightly.

Even so, it wouldn't have been enough to save my stripper ass; he would have almost instantly recovered, but I gave a desperate yank with all my might and he jerked forward, leg going out from under him.

I fell diagonally backward, my wrist jerking free of his grip. Harlen, knife still half-raised, crashed into the widescreen. Glass shattered and the blade pierced something within the TV. A shower of sparks that would have done a 4th of July fireworks show proud exploded over him and filled the air like sizzling fireflies.

Harlen landed half-in, half-out of the TV set, shuddering, unable to free himself as arcs of electricity zipped up the blade and through his body. He started sizzling, smoking, little bursts of flame snapping across his ragged body. An odor of seared rotted meat and ozone assailed my nostrils. Smoke billowed. As he began to dissolve, the knife dropped from his hand. Well, actually, the hand fell off first, if you want to get technical.

I scrambled backward, my spine slamming into the couch, and watched as the rest of what had been Carlis Harlen blackened and dissolved into nothingness. Moments later the widescreen was on fire and Harlen was gone. I hoped this time forever.

I realized the damn house was going to burn down if I didn't do something and forced myself up, despite the fact my legs shook like yesterday's spaghetti. I kicked the TV cord from the wall socket, then ran for the fire extinguisher. It took me a few minutes to get the fire out. Afterward, I dropped the extinguisher and collapsed to my knees, shaking so hard I couldn't get up for half an hour.

EPILOGUE

Tears ran down my face, half from fear, half from relief. It took me another fifteen minutes to regain enough composure to move. White foam bubbled throughout the widescreen's smoking guts and on the floor in front of TV amongst the shards of glass lay a blackened blade and the only other thing left of Carlis Harlen, a ring on a chain.

I crawled over to the ring and picked it up as if were a dead mouse. Harlen was gone and I had the ring back, and I still wasn't entirely sure how it had happened. My mind felt numb, but despite that fact I decided I wasn't going to give the ring to Lansing, at least not yet. She wanted it bad enough, maybe she would give me information on my sister. At any rate I would need to talk to Arly about it when he got back.

Arly. Oh, crap. I owed him another widescreen. That was the second one I'd managed to destroy in a little over two weeks. This Evil-chasing business was starting to get expensive.

But it was better than ending up on a slab.

I got to my feet, wondering where the cat had gotten off to. I was going to have to give him an extra can of Fancy Feast for his little act tonight. He deserved it.

Still shaky, I tucked the ring into my right jeans pocket, then went to the phone and started dialing. I needed Arly to come back tonight. I didn't want to sleep alone. Or with just the cat.

After I hung up twenty minutes later, I assured myself he had taken it as well as I could have expected. You know how those hero types are when they're not around to save their damsel's ass.

Speaking of which, it was time to feed the kitty.

THE TROUBLE WITH FLAPPERS

The old deserted house that's supposed to be haunted is one of those clichés you always see in old black and white movies or hear on Old Time Radio shows. You know the story: the hero's car breaks down on a dark and stormy night and said hero is forced to knock on the door of a creepy old mansion—the knocker's always a wolf's head or gargoyle face or some such thing—then gets sucked into some horrible nightmare.

Well, sometimes clichés are clichés for a good reason: because they happen.

I'd like to say it was a dark and stormy night, but it wasn't. It was mid-afternoon and the sun had that kind of frosty look it sometimes gets on brisk fall days. It made the boughs of evergreens lining either side of the road look like chilly emerald and glinted from maple, oak and birch leaves, which were ablaze with red, gold and orange. It made the stretch of road leading into New Salem, Maine more forlorn somehow, more lonely.

I'd been visiting a friend in Dark Harbor for the better part of the day and had been on the road about an hour when my cherry-red Beretta started to make the kind of engine sounds that sent bolts of electricity through my nerves and caused unladylike words to fly out of my mouth. Gurgling, gobbling sounds. Those were never good.

The Beretta's front tires hit a pothole and my teeth clacked together. That pissed me off even more, because the last thing I needed was to take out an axle or screw up the alignment. But as it turned out it didn't really matter because a half mile farther on the engine sputtered, shuddered and conked out.

Crap on a cracker.

After coasting to the side of the road and letting loose a few more choice words Arly would have been shocked to learn I knew, I got out of the car. Anger getting the better of me, I kicked a tire and swore I was going to trade the frickin' thing in. It had given me nothing but problems lately and was getting too old to find parts for anyway. I had kept it for sentimental reasons, but reliability was making a better argument.

I'm not even sure why I got out of the car. I had this harebrained idea I was going to look under the hood—like I'd know what the hell I was looking at. A monkey would have had a better chance of fixing it.

A monkey.

A chill streaked down my spine and I glanced around just in case my car breaking down was Bob's fault—or M-S Lansing's—but the little turd was nowhere to be seen this time. That was a switch. Bob usually managed to show his furry little ass every time something supernatural went wrong in my life. But this was nothing otherworldly, was it? This was just my damn clunky car crapping out on me and sticking me out in the middle of nowhere.

With a sigh, I grabbed my jean backpack from the seat and rummaged through it for my cell phone. It made an irritating chime as I flipped it open, but right now everything was grating on my nerves. This road was little traveled and I was still miles out of town, so walking wasn't something to look forward to.

I didn't think it was possible, but a moment later I got even more tweaked. No service, my stupid phone told me for no particular reason other than to get my panties in a tighter bunch. I was going to have words with the service rep who'd sold me this piece of crap when I got back to New Salem. I would have run it over with my car, had the damn thing been running.

"Great," I muttered, then frowned and shoved the phone back into my backpack. Looking about, I noticed the woods ended to one side about a hundred yards south of me. I flung the car door shut and started in that direction, knowing I was in for a long walk, but hoping there'd be a house somewhere along the way, one with a phone.

I got my wish, at least the house part, but my stripper sense went off with a clang, making me think of another cliché: be careful what the hell you wish for.

The place was huge, a Victorian style mansion, but run down. Weeds and unclipped hedges had overgrown the grounds and a few deadfalls littered the outskirts of the property. A stone driveway that led to a huge front porch spanning three-quarters of the house had grass poking through cracks and some of the stones were dislodged while others were missing completely.

Paint was chipped and peeling, while shutters hung loose in places and broken windows mocked me. A feeling washed through me, something dark, lonely, a sense of desolation and life passed. Nobody lived here; the place was deserted. That made the chances of a working phone about as likely as me fixing the car, but like an idiot I walked up the driveway anyway.

I could only imagine what this house might have been like in its heyday. Lavish parties, probably with smuggled booze during Prohibition—New Salem's shore caves and tunnels had been a haven for that sort of activity in the '20s. Stutz Bearcats would have lined the driveway and fancy women dripping with diamonds and gentlemen smoking expensive cigars would have been standing about chatting and looking important.

Did I ever tell you I have a pretty active imagination? Arly says I should have been a writer instead of a stripper; maybe that's another reason I started my journal.

I reached the door and sure enough, a gargoyle brass knocker. I banged it, knowing better, but doing it anyway.

A tingle zipped through my fingers and I jerked my hand away from the knocker. Despite my bulky blue sweater, I shuddered. Something twisted in my belly, some kind of...what?

I wasn't sure. Dread, maybe. Fear, possibly. Bad news, definitely.

No one came to the door and for some reason that surprised me, though I knew better. I had started to think of those old movies and radio shows again and half expected Boris Karloff or Vincent Price to open the door.

But nope, nothing. I was just about to turn and leave when a sound stopped me. I listened, another chill shivering through me. The wind whined a little through the trees, along with something else, hushed whispers, maybe, but I wasn't completely sure I heard that. What I was completely sure about was the music. Old music, like the kind played in speakeasies that flappers used to dance to.

"What the hell?" I muttered, my grip on my jean backpack tightening.

The music came from inside, distant, haunting somehow. I banged the knocker again. Maybe there was somebody here after all, and if they had music, then maybe they had a phone.

"Hello?" I yelled when nobody came. "My car broke down. I need to use your phone if you have one."

The door swung open. Just like in those old movies. It creaked like a frickin' coffin lid rising and nobody was behind it when it stopped.

You'd think with all the supernatural things Arly and I have run into in New Salem I'd be more used to creepy things, but I wasn't. It still gave me a sick feeling, though not sick enough to stop me from doing the worst possible thing I could do under the circumstances—walk into the foyer.

I really need to think more before I act. It's gotten me into trouble before and I had little reason to think it wouldn't again. And one of these times it was going to be permanent trouble, like dead trouble.

The foyer was gloomy, the chandelier gauzed in cobwebs and skittering spiders. I hugged my backpack tighter to me. A board creaked under my boots. A squeak came from somewhere and the memory of a certain demon fond of rats jumped into my mind. No, that particular demon was Helltoast, I reassured myself. It was only some animal that had gotten into the house and my yelling had probably scared it off. I hoped. I noticed the music had stopped, too.

A huge center stairway with carved banisters rose to a second level landing drenched in shadow. Webs and dust lay thick everywhere. I saw something scurry, something certainly big enough to be a rat and I really had no inclination to determine whether I was right.

"Hello?" I said again. It was s'posed to be a yell but it was more like a whimper. "Anybody here?" I waited a moment. "The door was open." My voice came a little louder this time. "I need to call a tow truck. Hello? Anyone?"

As if in response the music started again, a bit louder, and now I was sure it was real. It seemed to be coming from behind the closed double doors of a huge drawing room to my right. Everything inside me told me opening those doors was a piss poor idea. But you know I was going to do it anyway.

I moved towards them, my gaze sweeping about and as I reached the doors, I paused, listening again. Charleston. The music made me think of flappers dancing the Charleston and the Roaring 20s. I hoped the roaring part wasn't going to be a literal thing.

"Why are you here? You're not the one she picked."

I let out one of those mouse-running-across-your-feet yips and wondered if my heart was going to jump out of my mouth. The voice had come from behind me and I turned and saw her, a little girl standing before the staircase. She was dressed like a miniature flapper, right down to the fringed skirt, feathered headband and beads dangling about her small neck. Her blue eyes were somehow the saddest I had ever seen.

"My mommy wouldn't want you here, missy," the little girl said, her voice touched with an indescribable melancholy.

"I'm sorry, the door came open when I knocked." I took a step towards her and she didn't move, just kept looking at me with those sad eyes. "My car broke down and I was wondering if I could use your phone?"

Was that a smile that flickered across the little girl's face? Not quite, I decided. Something else. Less friendly.

The little girl's face, I noticed now, appeared almost bloodless. Great, another cliché, white as a ghost, crossed my mind. I quickly got rid of it.

"Are your parents in there?" I asked her, ducking my chin at the drawing room doors.

She nodded, the weird little not-a-smile flickering across her pale lips again.

"Are they having a costume party or something?"

"No..." the little girl said. "No costumes."

"But you're dressed...never mind." It didn't matter. All that mattered was finding out if they had a working phone before it got dark. Already the sunlight outside was waning and the inside of the place was even more gloomy than it had been a few minutes earlier.

I looked back at the doors, wondering if I should just go in and talk to the little girl's parents instead of wasting time out here. The whole thing was giving me a good case of the creeps.

When I turned back to the little girl I almost let out another yip. She was no longer there. I should have spent more time puzzling on how she could have possibly come and gone without making a sound on the creaking floorboards, but I was too intent on finding a phone and ignoring the dread building inside me. The music suddenly stopped again. Ok, I thought, time to see who was playing musical flapper chairs.

I went to the doors and pulled them open, hoping that I could just call Arly and get the hell out of here.

That didn't happen. Because what I saw inside the room froze me where I stood and I think my legs would have buckled and sent me to the floor had I not been gripping one of the doors so tight.

Two bodies, a man and a woman, both dressed in 1920s' costumes, lay sprawled on the floor. A bullet had shattered half the woman's face and another had punched a nice big gory cavern into the man's chest. Scarlet soaked the ornate carpet. The woman's dead hand clutched a gun. Her face, even in death, held the most horrible look of spite I had ever seen...

I turned away, my stomach threatening to come up with the Mandarin chicken salad I'd eaten for lunch. *This isn't real*, I wanted to tell myself. *It couldn't be.* I always wanted to tell myself that, but it never really worked out, so I'm not sure why I even bothered. It didn't work this time, either. My stomach still wanted out and it was all I could do to hold it down. An indescribable sensation went through me. Although I still wasn't used to things that go bump in the night, I was even less used to finding gruesomely murdered bodies. I suppose I could take some small comfort in the fact that at least these hadn't been chopped up into pieces and stuffed into a garbage bag like the one I'd found on Arly's porch last Christmas.

The little girl's face flashed through my mind; she'd looked so pale. Had she seen the bodies? Had she been in here with them? Were they her parents? And who had played the music? Why wasn't there anyone else around? Had the killer fled and left the little girl alive for some unknown reason?

But the gun was in the dead woman's hand...

Maybe the killer had planted it there? I wished Arly was with me; he was the detective.

I didn't get to think about it any longer because suddenly the Charleston music blared all around me again and I swear I jumped three feet out of my skin, then landed back in it. I spun, my mouth dropping open like I was Ms. Pac-Man. The bodies had vanished and the carpet was clean of blood. People swirled through the room now, all dressed in flapper dresses and swanky suits. On a corner table sat an old Victrola, one of those things with a big external horn, pumping out scratchy dance music—pumping it out loud enough to jangle every nerve in my shaking body. A mahogany bar flanked the east wall and razors of light, a peculiar sepia light, sliced through the huge bay windows and fell across the carpet in an eerie jagged pattern. In a corner, a couple was as close as humanly possible without being grafted together. His hands were all over her ass, hauling up her dress far enough to see most of her pale thin leg. Her hands were…eww. Nevermind where her hands were but she should have been asking him to cough. Their mouths were just about devouring each other's and I don't think I have ever seen that much tongue short of a KISS video.

Others danced the Charleston, arms and legs flying out at angles that would have made a chiropractor salivate. Everyone appeared blissfully unaware of my presence and I wondered if they could see me. Had I stepped back in time or was I witnessing some kind of residual haunting? Well, peachy, just when I thought I had a simple car break down I was right back in the middle of the supernatural again. I couldn't win.

The question of whether anyone could actually see me was answered an instant later.

"Hey, there, bubcat!" A voice came from my side at the same moment someone grabbed my arm and I almost went through the ceiling. A fire blazed in my eyes as I jerked my arm away, but any anger I might have used to my advantage dissolved the instant I looked into the face of the man standing beside me—the very same man I had seen lying I a pool of his own blood just a few moments ago!

His suit fit him like it was draped over a hanger and the watch chain dangling from the pocket gave him an effected air that looked pretty silly when you took into account the seedy look of his features. Class meets crass, as Arly liked to say. His pomaded hair was parted in the middle and slicked back, and one of those greasy slivers of a mustache you see in old silent movies perched over his lips. You know, the Snidely Whiplash type. The thought eased my shock but not much. Dark half circles nested beneath his brown eyes and his cheeks appeared drawn, his skin pocky.

He seemed momentarily taken aback after I wrenched my arm free, then raised both hands. "Easy-easy, there sweet bubs, don't cast a kitten. Just trying to make your acquaintance. You're a real bearcat. I like that." He tired to touch my arm again and I backed up a step. I didn't much care for the lascivious glint in his dull eyes—my guess is that he was on something more than alcohol from the looks of them, too. It reminded me of the look some of the drunks got at the Lagoon when I was swinging my girls around. But at the Lagoon that was one of the hazards of the job. I didn't have to put up with it here.

"Bubcat?" I said, my brow cinching, some of the anger coming back.

He flashed me a grin that said he wanted to get in my pants. Some things were timeless and guys thinking with their master cylinder was one of them.

It dawned on me, then, and with a bang. I wasn't wearing my jeans anymore, was I? Because a slight coolness whisked across my legs and as my head lowered I noticed a short dress that came to just above my knees and rolled stockings that stopped just below. I had on some kind of ugly boot things, too. Multi-colored beads dangled around my neck and some constraining garment flattened my breasts beneath a chemise. My hand went to my forehead, touching first a beaded headband, then my hair, which now felt like it was chopped in some sort of a bob, and there might have been a feather sticking out of my headband. I plucked it loose. Yup, it was a feather.

"What the hell—?" I muttered. I was a frickin' flapper! Oh, crap on a cracker. You had to be kidding me! And I stood out from the rest of the women in the room because flappers tended to be on the boyish side and I had far too many curves for that.

I noticed his gaze glued to my chest and it dawned on me what "bubs" were and now I was pissed off all over again. I think I liked this guy better when he was dead, and I suddenly understood why somebody might want to make him that way.

"Who are you?" I asked, as much venom in my voice as I could manage. I jammed the feather into his outer suit coat pocket.

He grinned, fished a flat silver case from inside his suit coat, selected a cigarette and popped it into his mouth. After returning the case to his pocket, he pulled out a match and lit the thing, then flung the stick on the carpet—real bright idea, that. I wondered why the house hadn't burned to the ground with that kind of stupidity. He ran his seamy little gaze up and down my flappered self.

Normally I'm pretty cool with guys looking at me. I'm a stripper, after all, and as I have said in a way it gives me power over them. *Most* of them. But not this guy. I didn't like this guy looking at me even fully, if oddly, clothed and I was about to make that plain by cramming my fist down his throat.

I did tell you Arly calls me impulsive, right? My impulse was to castrate this guy.

"Why, I'm the darb, my good girl, and that's no bushwa. A real cake-eater, if I do say so myself. I own this joint and since you're such a peach I figure we can hit on all six, if you know what I mean, Jelly-bean."

Cake-eater? Darb? Bushwa?I had no idea what he meant and I got the distinct feeling I didn't want to know.

"I didn't understand a word you just said, Mister..." I put a lot of bitch kitty in my voice, so even Mr. Full-of-Himself would get the drift. "But I understand body language and yours is telling me you better—what was the phrase back then?—oh yeah, go chase yourself."

His brow furrowed with a look that said he couldn't believe I was giving him the brush off. "Sheesh, what's your beef, bubs? Why you castin' me the bum's rush?"

"You call me bubs one more time and you'll find out." My eyes narrowed. I was really hitting pissed-off mode.

"Hey, there, Brooks, let's get a wiggle on..." The words came from another young woman who suddenly sidled up to the man and slipped her arm around his. A boyish young thing, she had plastered on enough makeup to shame a clown and her eyes said she'd spent way to much time with Dr. Opium, or whatever the hell it was they smoked back then.

"Yeah, yeah, my poor little bunny," he said, still ogling my girls. "This bubcat's all applesauce anyway." His voice carried a note of industrial annoyance; he was entirely too used to getting his way with women and that I wasn't responding to his charms really twisted his crank.

"What'd I say about that word?" I glared, ready to jam a finger into one of his eyes. He apparently thought better of pissing me off any further because he let the girl lead him away by the arm.

It was just about to come crashing in on me that I had just talked to a man I had seen dead just a few minutes earlier and that I was somehow stuck in a 1920s party wearing flapper clothes, when I noticed a woman glaring at me. She was leaning against the bar, the spite I had seen on her dead face now in blazing crimson on her living one. Her eyes narrowed, and her mouth drew into one of those lines women get whenever they catch their husbands watching my act at the Lagoon. Oh yeah, she was hurling all that eye venom straight at yours truly. I spread my hands and shrugged. I wasn't sure what else to do but the broad had been clasping a gun when I first saw her. Dead, but holding a gun just the same, so I wanted to make sure she didn't have it tucked somewhere in her little flapper panties now. Or whatever they wore back then. I wasn't about to lift my dress and look.

"They are going to kill her after…" a little girl's voice came from beside me. I whirled, getting damn tired of coming out of my skin every five minutes. Such was the life of a ghost-chasing stripper, Arly had told me, but I wasn't getting any more comfortable with the supernatural always having its nose up my ass.

"What?" I said, my gaze dropping to the little girl, the same little girl I had seen when I first entered the house, except now her face was no longer pale, though it still had the saddest look. Somehow it made me think of Pat, my sister, that day the home had separated us and I'd watched her leaving.

"You're not the one she picked. That's why my mommy looked at you that way. Only girls she's picked."

My brow furrowed. "Your mommy…is that your mommy over there, at the bar?"

The little girl nodded, her headband feather bobbing, then pointed to the boyish tweak adorning Mr. Full-of-Himself's arm. "She likes that kind of girl."

It dawned on me, then. Mommy Flapper liked to swing both ways and she liked them boyish. Daddy Dude, however, was looking for a chick with a little more front porch.

I looked over to see the woman had gone over to the man and his boyish companion. She was touching the young woman's arm, leaning in, drink in one hand, cigarette in a plastic holder in the other. I got the impression she was poising for a kiss and my stomach clenched. Mr. Darb, or whatever he had called himself, had a crap-eating grin on his face and was feeling up Miss Boy-O's skinny little fanny.

I turned the little girl away from them, wondering just what the hell they were thinking doing this in front of her. I wasn't a parent, and a hell of a lot of people knowing my profession probably wouldn't have wanted me to be one, but I knew children didn't need to be exposed to some things until they were a whole lot older than this girl and naughty sex games was one of them.

"It's ok," she said, the sadness in her eyes leaking into her voice. "They do it all the time. Then mommy kills them and daddy puts them in the ground out back, near the woods."

My eyes widened and shocked jumped across my face. I suddenly forgot everything else about my strange slip through time or whatever was happening here.

"She kills them?"

The little girl nodded and a tear wandered down her face. "They told me never to tell. Mommy doesn't like the girls after they are done doing what they do."

I almost slipped and asked her what it was they did, but looking back to the couple I already knew the answer. The woman leaned in further and tried to kiss the girl. Apparently this girl wasn't quite high enough to let that happen and slapped the woman. Freakin' hard, too. I heard it above the music and so did a number of the other guests.

The slap changed things, perhaps put the endgame into motion. I'm not sure, but everyone else in the room disappeared. I mean, just, frickin' poof, gone. Everybody except the happy dead couple and the girl they were trying to wrangle into the 1920s version of Naked Twister.

The woman's face washed bloodless with fury and she dropped her cigarette and drink, then shoved the young woman. The girl fell back and Mr. Darb started babbling something, then gesturing towards me. I knew that wasn't a good sign.

"I have to go, now, missy."

I glanced at the little girl and she gave me that odd not-a-smile.

"No, sweetie, you come with me. We'll get somebody to come here and stop this. You shouldn't be seeing things like this." Exactly what "this" was, I wasn't sure. For all I knew I was watching ghosts and DHS really didn't have much in place to deal with that option.

I reached for her hand but she pulled back. Her eyes grew sadder, reminding even me more of Pat. "I can't, missy. I just wanted some-body to know. I'm tired of being here. I've been here such a long time." The girl tried a smile, then looked down at her middle. "I'm bleeding…"

"What?" I whispered.

She had clasped her hands over her belly and blood bubbled be-tween her fingers. I reached out for her but she had already started towards the couple. The other young woman had vanished and the music suddenly stopped.

The man gestured at me again and now the woman was gesturing too and it wasn't nice gesturing. In fact, I was a little surprised that kind of gesturing was around in the '20s.

Miss Flapper Mom took a few steps towards me, reaching a spot near the door when the man grabbed her arm. She yanked her arm away, rage turning her face purple, and her hand darted beneath her dress.

Oh, just crap. She did have the gun. And she pulled it out.

A shocked expression jumped onto the man's face and he sobered immediately.

"What the hell do you think you are you doing?" he snapped at her.

She glared, hand shaking. Shaking hands holding guns freaked me out. "I told you, *I* pick them!"

He spread his hands. "Ish kabibble, doll, sure you do. Don't cast a kitten."

She looked at me, spite swimming in her eyes. She was clearly hopped up on something, irrational.

"Him and his goddamn stupid lingo…" She shook her head. "I'm so tired of being this way…" Genuine bitterness laced her tone, deep, unfathomable, even. "So goddamn tired. He never wanted me, you know. He knocked me up, that's why he married me. Then he wanted…others…lots of others. I gave in, as long as they looked like boys. I even convinced myself I liked it for awhile. I got to choose. But I had to watch them with him, too, so they had to die. You do understand?"

The little girl had stopped a few feet from them, staring intently at her parents. Tears trickled down her face.

I shook my head. "No, I don't understand. You should have left him. You should have protected your child from this." I was surprised at how angry my tone came out but I had seen too many girls in my profession come from abusive backgrounds and grow old before their years. I knew how lives were ruined by parents who didn't give a damn about anything but their own selfishness needs.

She shrugged. "Times were different, then, Peaches. A wife just didn't leave…"

Then, her gaze shifting back to the man, she aimed the gun and pulled the trigger.

At the moment she swung the gun towards her father, the little girl screamed and jumped forward.

"No, Daaaddddyyy!"

All emotion stopped inside me and I was afraid I was going to black out. I couldn't move, couldn't stop what was happening, and everything inside me screamed *nooo!* in impotent mocking silence.

The little girl's body flew backward and crashed to the floor, five feet away. The woman just stood there, shock raping her face, all color bleeding out. The man whirled, horror in his eyes. He ran to the little girl, who now lay on the carpet, and knelt over her. His hands trembled as he reached out, touched her small shoulder, then drew back.

"No, oh Christ, no." He turned his face back to the mother, who hadn't budged. "You stupid bitch! You stupid, stupid bitch..." Tears rushed from his eyes. And from mine. They streamed down my face because I knew that little girl was dead, and I knew she had been dead when I entered the house and that she was showing me this for a reason. I could not prevent what happened, because it had happened decades ago and was merely playing itself out like an old movie with a tragic ending. She had just wanted me to know. To witness. But I didn't want to. I wanted to close my eyes and wash the image of her death from my mind. But I couldn't. I would never be able to. It would be a part of my nightmares until the day I died.

I turned and hurled onto the sofa. I must have retched for a good five minutes, but it felt like days. When I wiped my mouth on my arm I was back in my sweater and jeans and the man was leaping at the woman, murder now on his face. In his own weird way he cared about that little dead girl, his daughter. He just hadn't cared enough the right way.

Spite and rage swept away the woman's shock, and tears rushed from her eyes. "You made me do it, you bastard! It's *your* goddamn fault."

She pulled the trigger and the man shuddered in his tracks, a gaping cavern opening in his chest. Blood splattered his suit coat and chin. He collapsed, lay still. Then the woman gazed at me, raised the gun to her head."

"*Don't!*" I yelled, my hand going out, knowing it would do no good.

The shot took off half her face and she crumpled, hand still clenching the gun.

My legs went soupy and I grabbed the edge of the sofa so I wouldn't go down. The shot still reverberated through the room, echoed in my mind, and I couldn't get the sight of the little girl's body out of my head.

"It's all right, missy…" a voice came and I looked up. The little girl stood there, looking forlorn and sad, but somehow more at peace than she had the first time I had seen her. The bodies had disappeared and the room was now full of cobwebs and dead stillness, gloom. It was a room of death, of the dead, of lives never really lived.

"Your mother, she…"

The girl nodded. "I just wanted somebody to know what happened. I've been waiting all his time. It's been so lonely here. But now I can…go…"

She went. Just like that. Didn't fade like a ghost, just went like somebody had spliced together a filmstrip poorly.

I thought for an instant I heard music, very distant, very echoy, flapper music, but I couldn't be sure, because I did something pretty unbrave.

I ran like hell.

***

A week later I still couldn't get the memory of that little girl out of my head. Her face haunted me, her life haunted me. I had walked miles that day to call a tow truck and have Arly come pick me up. I had asked him to check with Sturdevant to see what he could dig up about the house and whoever had lived there.

It was on the books, listed as a suicide and an unsolved double disappearance. Only the woman's body had been found, dead by her own hand. It had been assumed the husband had taken off with the daughter, leaving her despondent.

Things hadn't occurred quite the way I had witnessed them, from the sounds of the report, at least not in the same time sequence. Because no mention had been made of the man or little girl having been murdered. But when they dug up the back yard near the woods after I told Arly what the girl said about burying the young women, they'd discovered both the little girl and her father's remains, pending tests, along with bones from a number of different bodies.

Apparently the mother had dragged the bodies of her husband and child to the edge of the property and buried them before killing herself. I don't know exactly what she was thinking, or not thinking, what her motive might have been, but maybe she wanted everybody to assume he had run off with the daughter, that they were all right somewhere. Maybe she thought in her deranged mind that somehow absolved her of some of the guilt. Maybe she simply didn't want her depraved life-style uncovered and bringing shame to any family members she might have left among the living. Or maybe the burden of being forced into being a goodtime girl and committing acts she'd initially abhorred had simply cracked her mind. Who knew?

That was the trouble with flappers…it was hard to tell.

Don't forget to read the novel that started it all for our gal:

Grimm
by
Howard Hopkins

Available at fine online bookstores everywhere...

ABOUT THE AUTHOR

Howard Hopkins lives in a small Maine seacoast town and has written thirty westerns under his penname Lance Howard, the latest of which saw print in August, 2008, titled, *The Devil's Rider*. In addition, he's written seven horror novels under his own name as well as three children's horror novels in *The Nightmare Club* series, comic book scripts, short stories and articles for various publications. He recently co-edited *The Avenger Chronicles* and adapted The Spider into graphic novel format for Moonstone Books. Visit his webpage at: http://www.howardhopkins.com.

And don't forget to check out Chloe's personal journal, The Chloe Files Online, at http://chloefiles.blogspot.com for the latest Chloe updates.

Also by Howard Hopkins...

Grimm
The Chloe Files #1: Ashes to Ashes
The Nightmare Club #1: The Headless Paperboy
The Nightmare Club #2: The Deadly Dragon
The Nightmare Club #3: The Willow Witch
Night Demons
Dark Harbors
The Dark Riders
Pistolero

Lance Howard Westerns...

Blood on the Saddle
The Comanche's Ghost
Blood Pass
The West Witch
Wanted
Ghost-town Duel
The Gallows Ghost
The Widow Maker
Guns of the Past
Palomita
The Last Draw
The Deadly Doves
The Devil's Peacemaker
The West Wolf
The Phantom Marshall
Bandolero
Pirate Pass
The Silver-mine Spook
Ladigan
Vengeance Pass
Johnny Dead
Poison Pass
Ripper Pass
Nightmare Pass
Hell Pass
Haunted Pass
Desolation Pass
Blood Creek
The Devil's Rider
Coyote Deadly

www.ingramcontent.com/pod-product-compliance
Lightning Source LLC
Chambersburg PA
CBHW032011240626
47153CB00003B/1215